D0380658

TRISHA LEAVER
LINDSAY CURRIE

HARDWIRED

Genetically Flawed,

Perfectly

Human

flux®
Woodbury, Minnesota

Glenrock Branch Library
Box 1000
Glenrock, WY 82637

39092 08802357 9

Hardwired © 2015 by Trisha Leaver and Lindsay Currie. All rights reserved. No part of this book may be used or reproduced in any manner whatsoever, including Internet usage, without written permission from Flux, except in the case of brief quotations embodied in critical articles and reviews.

First Edition
First Printing, 2015

Book design by Bob Gaul
Cover design by Lisa Novak
Cover images by iStockphoto.com/19619906/©MACIEJ NOSKOWSKI
            iStockphoto.com/21415931/©luismmolina
Interior art by iStockphoto.com/12100830©macida

Flux, an imprint of Llewellyn Worldwide Ltd.

This is a work of fiction. Names, characters, places, and incidents are either the product of the author's imagination or are used fictitiously, and any resemblance to actual persons living or dead, business establishments, events, or locales is entirely coincidental. Cover model used for illustrative purposes only and may not endorse or represent the book's subject.

Library of Congress Cataloging-in-Publication Data
Leaver, Trisha, author.
   Hardwired/Trisha Leaver, Lindsay Currie.—First edition.
      pages cm
   Summary: After several months in a government facility undergoing psychological testing related to his "warrior gene," seventeen-year-old Lucas has been approved to return to normal life—but decides instead to go back into the facility to save a prisoner and reveal what is truly going on there.
   ISBN 978-0-7387-4226-7
[1. Science fiction. 2. Genetics—Fiction.] I. Currie, Lindsay, author. II. Title.
   PZ7.L428Har 2015
   [Fic]—dc23

                                                     2015023108

Flux
Llewellyn Worldwide Ltd.
2143 Wooddale Drive
Woodbury, MN 55125-2989
www.fluxnow.com

Printed in the United States of America

DEC 1 5 ENT'D

Also by Trisha Leaver and Lindsay Currie

Creed

To the Fearless Five, for their continued love and support!

The Rhode Island Herald
November 8, 2015

The mugging at the bus stop. The shooting at the mall. The carjacking downtown. All random acts of violence considered unstoppable until now. After more than a decade of research, the Institute for Genetic Testing (IGT) claims to have found definitive proof that carriers of the MAOA-L gene are genetically predisposed to violence.

The MAOA gene, commonly referred to as the warrior gene, has been at the center of controversy for several years as researchers tried to make a correlation between antisocial behavior and the gene that codes for monoamine oxidase A. Recently, while testing several high-profile criminals in search of a common genetic link, IGT scientists identified MAOA-L. The discovery of this genetic link will enable law enforcement officers to identify potential offenders *before* they engage in violent criminal behavior.

In an unprecedented move, President Conway, after consulting with the Government Task Force for Violent Crimes, signed an executive order mandating the testing of all adolescents on their seventeenth birthday. Those teens testing positive for MAOA-L will be held in a secure facility for two months, where they will undergo a series of psychological screenings to determine their potential for sociopathic behavior. The construction of twelve state-of-the-art testing facilities is underway, the first one slated to open this spring in Vermont.

ONE

The strobe light above my bed jarred me awake. Its irritatingly bright light was accompanied by an equally annoying buzz that broke through the brief three-minute dream I'd drifted into. A dream about a world where Tyler was alive and I wasn't trapped inside a concrete shoebox at the mercy of some geneticist's whims.

I looked up at the circular contraption, thinking of all the destructive ways I could kill it but never planning to act on any of them. Violence was the reaction IGT's scientists were hoping for, the one reaction that would get me condemned forever.

The thin pillow they'd gifted me did little to block the light, but I yanked it from beneath my head and slapped it over my eyes anyway. You'd think after three nights, I'd be used to their latest form of torture—sleep deprivation—but no. Every time the blasted thing flared to life, I'd shoot out of bed, my feet hitting the cold tile floor as I willed my heart to stop racing. Adrenaline coursed through me, making me edgy, irritable, and ready to lash out at anybody and everything. A few more nights of that, and they'd win. I'd lose what little control I had left and snap, turning myself into the violent threat I swore I'd never become.

"Shit, man, get it together." Frustrated, I jumped down from the top bunk and dropped my head to my knees, forcing my breathing to slow. It didn't work. It never did.

The temperature in our room was jacked up to over 80 degrees. Sweat poured off my body, trickling into my eyes and screwing with my already hazy vision. I didn't know how much longer I could take this. Three nights of being jolted awake every thirteen minutes and seven seconds had me seriously contemplating giving up. At least locked away in a cell surrounded by darkness and silence, I would've been able to sleep.

Chris grunted and flopped over on the bottom bunk, then settled back into the mattress and started snoring again. I watched him for a minute, jealousy flooding my system. He'd obviously found a way to block out the lights, not even flinching as they flashed above us in a blinding crescendo of torment. I needed to figure out how he did it, bribe him if need be, perhaps with my dessert at meals or the magazine I'd smuggled in. Either way, Chris was going to tell me how he'd managed to sleep through this latest test or it was going to be his face and not the flashing light above my bed that I took my anger out on.

The room went blissfully silent, but flashes of silver and white still streaked my vision, each burst ratcheting up my anger. The lights always lasted longer than the noise. Like a tease . . . a way to poke at us for a few more seconds.

I straightened up and stared at my bunk. I hated the hard-won comfort it offered. Our beds were sparse—a mattress, a blanket, and a flattened pillow. We'd had sheets when we first got here; that is, until the guy across the hall figured out how to tie his into a noose. I don't think the staff would've cared so much if he'd used it on himself. But he went after his roommate, left him dangling over the edge of the metal bedframe. Or so the rumors said.

I shook off that image, my eyes tracking the red light of the surveillance camera mounted in the corner of our room. It flashed twice then died out. It'd taken me a whopping twelve hours my first day to figure out the pattern. The camera would scan the room for five minutes and twenty-seven seconds, then the light would go off. We got two minutes and twelve seconds of surveillance darkness, then the red light would blink on, the watchful eyes of the Bake Shop's impotent guards recording our every move.

We lived for those brief two-minute stints each night when no one was watching and we could be ourselves. This place was dark and depressing, ate away at any hope you had. But at night, when silence surrounded us and you could trick your mind into thinking you were somewhere else, Chris and I would talk. Stupid little bursts of conversation gave us hope, reminded us that we had families and friends ... entire lives waiting for us back home.

I'd tried to ignore Chris at first, spent the better part of two days tuning out his questions. But with nothing but your own dark thoughts to keep you company at night, it got lonely pretty quick. It was either talk to him or lose my mind. In an attempt to stay sane, I broke down and told him on our third night here that I was the catcher for my high school's baseball team. Chris played left field for his high school team, and so the conversation started and kept going from there. We disagreed on everything, but those stupid arguments were what passed the time as we stumbled through one psychological torment after another.

But that night I was tired and irritated, not exactly thinking straight. I stood there silently watching the surveillance camera and timing my approach. Two cycles later, when the camera went dark, I made my move. I felt my way across the metal bedframe, slipping my hands under Chris's mattress. He mumbled something in his sleep and rolled over to face the wall. Good, it'd hurt that much more when I shoved him into it.

I took a deep breath and jerked one side of his mattress up, sending Chris tumbling into the wall. He wasn't hurt—I made sure to check my strength before I heaved him up and over—but he was definitely awake and just as irritated as me.

"What the hell, Lucas?" Chris grumbled as he rubbed his forehead.

He went to say something else, but I waved him off, jutting my chin in the direction of the camera. I'd been keeping time in my head and in less than five seconds, there'd be three sets of eyes watching our every move.

Not wanting the guards to question why I was out of my bunk, I moved over to the urinal affixed to the far wall. Chris sighed and played along, laying back against his pillow and pretending to be asleep.

"Off," Chris said, letting me know it was safe to turn around.

"You want to tell me how you've managed to sleep through that"—I paused only long enough to gesture to the light above my bunk; it was going off again, like a messed-up disco ball on speed—"for the past three nights?"

Chris gave me a blank stare, not hearing anything I'd said. I fought the urge to shake him, to take out all my exhaustion on his expressionless face. But Chris was the closest thing to a friend I had in here, the only person I trusted, and I needed him on my side.

"How. Are you. Sleeping. Through that?" I repeated my question, my words slow and exaggerated as I tried to rein in my frustration.

"What?" Chris nearly screamed the word at me, and for a second I feared I'd accidently done some real damage to his head when I'd shoved him into the wall. He sat up and cleared his eyes with the heels of his hand, then pulled out a small wad of paper from his right ear. He had earplugs in. Homemade earplugs.

He yanked the other plug out and dropped it to the bed. I picked it up, curious as to how he'd pulled it off. They looked like nothing more than balled-up pieces of paper, but to my knowledge, there wasn't any paper in this room. We didn't even have toilet paper in there. Piss all you wanted in the urinal bolted to the wall, but if you needed to take a dump, yeah ... best wait for morning when you had access to the communal bathrooms. God forbid they'd give the potentially unstable teens a newspaper or box of tissues.

I mean, if sheets could be used as a deadly weapon, imagine what kind of destructive device we could've made with something as lethal as toilet paper.

I shook my head in disgust. Nothing was allowed in our rooms that might've been deemed a distraction. Our only amusement was each other, and we all knew how well that had worked out across the hall.

"Where did you get this?" I asked, unfolding the paper. I could make out a few letters, but not enough to form any words, never mind give me a clue as to where'd he gotten a book.

"From the magazine you snuck in here and hid in your mattress," Chris said, at the exact same time I flipped the torn piece of paper over and glimpsed a fragment of the picture. It was my magazine all right, and if I was seeing straight, that was Miss January.

I scrunched the wads of paper back up and fitted them to my own ears. My *Playboy*, my ear plugs. "What about the light?" I asked. Noise aside, it was the light that bothered me most. It had a way of messing with my vision so badly that I wanted to claw my eyes out of my own head.

"That's all you." Chris chuckled as he settled back into his bed. "It's above your bunk, not mine. Your ass pretty much blocks it out."

Son of a bitch. Here I was, sleep-deprived and nursing a tumor-like headache, while he was sleeping like a baby, my *Playboy* shoved in his ears, my ass blocking his view of the strobe light. Not anymore. Now it was his time to suffer.

"Bottom bunk is mine for the next three days," I said as I wedged myself in between him and the wall.

"You're lucky I'm tired, Lucas. Otherwise I would kick your ass," Chris said as he snagged his pillow from beneath my head and stood up, his hands folded across his chest as if he was contemplating challenging me.

I laughed. "What's stopping you?"

"Them," he said, pointing to the camera. The red light was back on, a bunch of nameless guards waiting beyond it, probably hoping I'd finally popped. Chris let out a deep sigh, his hands relaxing at his sides. "Nothing would make them happier than me taking a swing at you."

I turned over, giving the camera my back, hating myself for flipping out on Chris, the only person I actually liked in this place. "I'm sorry," I said, feeling like an ass for having taken out my frustration on him. "I'm just so done with all their tests."

"Don't let them break you. Not like this," Chris said as he climbed up to the top bunk and tossed my pillow down to me. "We're nearly halfway done, Lucas. You lose it now, and they'll keep you locked up forever."

"I know," I replied as I rolled over and buried my head beneath the thin blanket. "You can have the bottom bunk tomorrow, and for the rest of the week if you want." He could have it for the remainder of our time in this place; I felt that bad about what I'd done. "I just need one night's sleep. Just one."

TWO

The electronic lock sealing us in our room chimed once, soft and low. It was a sound I both loved and despised. A fleeting surge of hope always accompanied that tiny noise, a promise of freedom that lasted no more than a few wasted seconds before reality set in. I wasn't being released; I was simply being moved to a larger cage.

Not waiting for Chris, I stepped out into the hall and flipped off the guard waiting for me. I could be as rude as I wanted to the guards. So long as I didn't physically go after them, they couldn't touch me. I'd learned that small yet useful fact from my brother, Tyler, and tested it out myself on my first day there. So far, his advice had proved solid.

"I thought you'd be excited about this next phase of testing." Ms. Tremblay, the facility-appointed shrink, stopped in front of the door to my room, her eyes darting between me and the guard I'd just given the finger to. "This is the first step in getting you back home to your friends and family, proving that you can become a valuable and constructive member of society."

I nodded rather than argued. I absolutely was excited about going home, but the idea that there was a life or friends waiting for my back in Foster, Rhode Island, was absurd. IGT's testing program had physically destroyed one-half of my family. And as for friends, they'd pretty much written me off the day my brother had tested positive for what I liked to call the "psychotically crazy gene." I could join the priesthood, fund a world charity, dedicate my life to saving the wombat population in Australia, and it wouldn't matter. This facility and their stupid genetic test had sealed my fate, and there was nothing that I could do or say to ever change that.

"So long as all goes well in these last two weeks of testing, Lucas, we can move you out to the reintegration facility and then back home," Ms. Tremblay continued. "You have your entire life in front of you. A clean slate."

This woman was either the dumbest person I'd ever met or the best liar. After passing the six-week "testing phase," I'd have two weeks of confinement at what they lovingly referred to as the "reintegration" facility—a fourteen-day-long study hall where they monitored us for delayed signs of stress. What Ms. Tremblay saw as a light at the end of the tunnel, I saw as fourteen more days for me to potentially screw up.

"Are you excited about returning home, Lucas?" she asked.

"Nothing worth going home to, ma'am," I said, refusing to give into her delusional optimism a second longer.

Ms. Tremblay paused, her normally stoic facade faltering. "Nobody? No friends? Sports? Girlfriend?"

I chuckled to myself. She knew exactly what was waiting

for me back home, probably had my entire life history committed to memory. Ms. Tremblay was fishing, trying to gauge my tolerance level outside these walls and wondering if there was a trigger at home she'd overlooked. That was her job, after all—determining if my genetic makeup predisposed me to criminal behavior. Not as a common criminal, but the violent, psychotic type that randomly opens fire in minimarts and crowded malls.

"None of the above," I replied, knowing full well whatever friends I had wrote me off the day I tested positive. And as for family, I had Tyler's grave as a constant reminder of what this place cost families like mine. They'd taken my brother two years ago, dragged him out of our house with nothing but the clothes on his back. Didn't seem right to me, even then—a star athlete who'd never done much more than TP a couple of houses on Halloween being hauled away like some kind of farm animal.

Tyler may have gone into the Bake Shop normal and well-adjusted, but something about the place changed him. Broke him. He quit the baseball team, quit school altogether the day he returned home. Refused to eat, refused to do anything but sit in his room and scribble notes in his journal. He'd sit on his bed and stare at his walls for day, not acknowledging anyone.

His girlfriend, Olivia, begged him to talk, to cry, to scream, to do anything other than sit there completely trapped in his own mind. She spent every waking hour in his bedroom trying to get through to him.

The one day she'd left him alone, the one time Olivia ventured home to shower and grab a change of clothes, everything changed. She'd asked me to watch him, said he was quieter than usual. I shrugged off Olivia's concerns; as far as I could tell, he was same closed-off person he'd been for the past two weeks. I'd left him alone for fifteen minutes tops to get Suzie off the bus. When I came back, Tyler was in the backyard, sitting in an old lawn chair by the circle of rocks we used for fires. I was psyched to see him out of his room. I called out his name, but he didn't answer, didn't even turn his head in my direction. At first I thought he was sleeping, but the minute I laid my hand on his shoulder, I knew.

His head rolled to the side, the bottle of pills he'd swallowed falling to the ground next to a bottle of whisky. I tried to revive him, slamming my fist into his chest and literally forcing my own breath into his lungs, but he just lay there, his eyes rolled back in his head, his arms hanging limply by his sides.

Tyler had survived their tests, proved that he wasn't some psychopath on the verge of exploding, and for what? Only to kill himself when he got home? It was so pointless. In a way, that was my biggest fear: that I'd survive this place only to crack at home. But I wouldn't let Ms. Tremblay know that.

I swore that day I'd make amends for what they did to Tyler. I'd beat their tests and survive, prove them wrong. This place wouldn't break me. For my brother's sake, I wouldn't let them.

"Lucas!" Ms. Tremblay's words cut through my thoughts. "Did you hear anything I said?"

"Every word," I lied. "But I didn't hear anything that warranted an answer."

She huffed her disappointment and started walking

down the hall. I followed her, well aware of the two guards flanking me. They were always there, crowding my space. I toyed with making a move just to screw with them but quickly decided against it. I hadn't gotten this far along only to piss it all away for my own sick satisfaction.

Ms. Tremblay stopped abruptly, her curt nod sending me to the wall where I lined up with the other guys from our wing.

Chris appeared next to me a second later and I scanned his forehead, breathing a sigh of relief. It actually looked pretty good, with virtually no sign of injury from me slamming him into the wall last night. Thank God, the last thing I needed was to be on the hook for losing my temper on the only friend I had in this place.

"Thanks for the headache," he whispered as we made our way toward the communal bathrooms.

"Sorry," I mumbled. I'd managed to get a solid four hours of sleep, thanks to his earplugs, and had woken up feeling physically great but still guilty as hell. "I meant what I said—bottom bunk is yours for the next week."

"Nope," Chris said, shaking his head. "Not if it means you losing it." He leaned closer, his voice so low that I could barely make out his words. "Besides, I made a new set of ear plugs last night after you went to sleep. What's the point of having that magazine if you're only going to hide it in your mattress and forget it's even there?"

I laughed. Chris was right. I hadn't looked at that magazine since the day I'd smuggled it in. I'd brought it with me solely to annoy the guards when they went through my bag. Funny, it only pissed me off more when they laughed and handed it back to me with a warning not to let Ms. Tremblay find it.

"What do you think they have planned for us today?" I asked, purposefully changing the subject.

Chris shrugged his shoulders and let out a tired breath. "Beats me. Probably more head games designed to see which one of us is going to break first."

"Won't be me," I mumbled to myself. "It won't be you either."

THREE

The room we entered was larger than the testing rooms and lined with couches and overstuffed chairs. The floor was carpeted, not tiled, and the walls were painted a soft yellow, not the crusty old gray that seemed to cover every surface of the facility. Even the security guard posted inside the door was dressed in plain clothes, with a friendly looking name-tag that read *Murphy*. But his casual appearance didn't fool me. Jeans and button-down shirt aside, he was armed.

I sank down into one of the chairs and stretched out, suddenly realizing how much I missed real furniture and longing for my own bed. Chris swatted my legs off the couch and sat down next to me, his glare telling me not to look so relaxed. He was right; that's what they wanted, that's what this room was—a comfortable place where they could trick you into letting your guard down. That wasn't going to happen.

"This is where the real fun starts," I said to Chris. "Where they try to get you to tell them all your deep, dark secrets."

"Says who?"

"Tyler," I replied. I'd slept in his room the night he died, foolishly trying to hang on to some tiny piece of him. It suddenly got cold, the old drafty window above his bed sending a chill through the room that had me shivering and searching for a blanket. When I shook out an old blanket I found on the top shelf of his closet, a composition book fell to the floor by my feet. The instant I picked it up, I knew what it was—his journal, tiny fragments of the time he'd spent in the Bake Shop. I read it from cover to cover that night; he gave me enough information to figure this place out. Enough information to scare me.

"You boys will be moving on to the reintegration phase shortly," Ms. Tremblay announced, her gaze sweeping across the ten of us sitting in the room. "No doubt you have some questions about what to expect, both there and at home. This is the time to discuss those issues, along with anything else you have on your minds."

I nudged Chris's arm, warning him to say nothing. He nodded, a half-smile parting his lips. He had no intention of giving them any information.

"Be assured," Ms. Tremblay continued when we all remained silent, "what is said in this room stays in this room. Nothing you confide in me or your peers will be mentioned in your discharge notes."

"Ha." The sharp remark was out of my mouth before I had a chance to stop it. All eyes, even those of the security guard, turned to me.

"Perhaps you would like to start, Lucas," Ms. Tremblay said.

Oh, I wanted to start all right. I wanted to curse Ms. Tremblay and this entire facility for what they'd done to my brother. I wanted to warn all the genetically flawed guys in here with me, Chris especially, that being sent home equated to nothing more than an isolated hell. Most of all, I wanted to tell Ms. Tremblay to take her fake smile and circle-of-trust crap and shove it. But I wasn't that dumb.

"Nope, I'm good," I lied. "Couldn't be better. Happy to be going home. Can't wait to see my family and friends, *ma'am*."

"You have the benefit of experience here, Lucas. Perhaps you'd like to share some of that with the others, maybe dispel some myths and rumors they may have heard."

"And how do you figure that? I've been locked up in this Bake Shop for the exact same amount of time they have," I said, and she rolled her eyes at my pet name for the facility. "I've suffered through the same tests and heard all the same excuses about how the entire gene-testing protocol is for the greater good."

She shook her head, aggravated that I wasn't coughing up my feelings. "You had a brother who came through this program two years ago, isn't that right?"

I nodded. That wasn't exactly earth-shattering information. It was in my intake file, along with my address and date of birth. "I have a dog named Brady and a sister named Suzie, too, but I don't see how any of that is their business," I said, fanning my hand out to encompass the other nine guys sitting in the room with me.

"I knew your brother," Ms. Tremblay replied, ignoring my sarcasm. "You remind me a bit of him. Strong-willed and determined."

I bit back my response. What she meant was stubborn and defiant. They'd really tried to break Tyler, spent a little more time on him than the others, or so I'd gathered from his journal. But he wouldn't crack. Not until he got home, anyway. Once he was back in his own bedroom, safe from their reach, he let go.

"My brother is dead," I said, purposely checking my emotions. He'd killed himself sixteen short days after he got home, choked down a fistful of pills right there in our own backyard.

"He's dead," I repeated. "And the way I see it, it's your fault."

Ms. Tremblay's breath shuddered to a stop, and I briefly wondered if she'd ever been told what happened to Tyler, if the flow of information coming into this place was as tightly controlled as the information going out.

"Dead," she whispered. "How? When?"

"Doesn't matter," I said. "He's gone, and talking about it in this little group session of yours isn't going to bring him back."

"No, but it may help you."

I shook my head. As far as I could tell, she was the one in charge of our testing, the one who decided which of us to ease up on and which to push harder. And now, what? Simply because the testing phase was two-thirds over, she figured she could just change hats, come at me like some kind, generous, social-worker-type person who wanted to make sure I was properly dealing with my brother's death? Screw that.

"I don't want your kind of help," I said. "I don't need it."

She sat there, silently staring at me as if trying to figure out what to say next. "All right, Lucas," she finally said. "If you don't want to talk about Tyler, then how about we talk about you?"

My mind circled back to the day I was taken from home, the day Sheriff Watts showed up, a warrant in hand for me to report to the intake facility that would process me for the Bake Shop. I wasn't so much worried about Mom; she'd known the odds of me testing positive were insanely high the second they'd taken Tyler. It was my baby sister Suzie I was worried about. She was three years old when Tyler died, barely even remembered him, but I'd been looking out for her since she was two, since the day Dad left and Mom had to go back to work to keep us fed and the mortgage paid.

"Be good, for Mom," I'd said to Suzie as I stood up.

"Where are you going?" she asked, her eyes darting toward the window and the three police cruisers waiting in our driveway.

I searched my brain for something to say, an explanation, a lie about where I would be. What I came up with was an overly stupid: "Camp."

Mom started crying, her small frame shaking as she clung to me. I didn't know what to say to make her feel better. The truth was, this sucked for her as much as me. I hadn't seen my father in three years, my brother was dead, and now they were taking me. And in eleven years they'd test Suzie.

I felt a sharp pain in my leg and looked down. Chris's foot was lodged in my shin as he painfully tried to coax me out of my thoughts and back to the room full of guys staring at me. Their bodies were tilted forward, elbows resting on their knees, waiting for me to deliver them some piece of wisdom. Unfortunately, I had nothing. Nothing they'd want to hear anyway.

"You know what, I do have something to say," I started, my eyes landing on every one of those guys as I spoke. "You no longer have a home. Everyone you thought you knew—your friends, your teachers, the girl you slept with for the past two years—they'll all turn on you. You'll see fear in their eyes and hear the words they whisper behind your back. Home, a normal life, a future … yeah, that's never going to happen. For any of us."

Their faces paled as the truth of my words settled in. I'd frightened them, taken away what little hope they were clinging to.

"If you have nothing useful to contribute, Lucas, perhaps I should move on to your roommate," Ms. Tremblay said, her forced smile back in place.

"Go right ahead," I said. I doubted Chris would tell her anything about his personal life, but if she needed to test that theory for herself, then I certainly wasn't going to stop her.

"Your father owns a security company, isn't that right, Chris?" Ms. Tremblay began, and Chris nodded, giving her nothing.

"And you're an avid hunter?" she continued.

The air in the room went from heavy to suffocating with

that question. Everyone shifted uncomfortably in their seats, their eyes darting between the door and the plain-clothes security guard still watching over us.

"You are aware that one of the stipulations of your release is that you can never own a firearm," the guard said from his position by the door.

"So I've been told," Chris muttered, and I couldn't help but smile. If either of them was trying to get a rise out of him, it wasn't working.

"And does that bother you?" Ms. Tremblay leaned forward in her seat, her gray eyes peeking over the rim of her glasses. "The idea that because you are an MAOA-L carrier, you can no longer engage in one of your favorite hobbies?"

Chris looked at me. The message he was silently communicating clear: *How far can I push them?*

"As far as you want," I mouthed back. As long as he stayed in his seat and didn't threaten anyone in this room, then he was safe. Besides, wasn't it just last week that Ms. Tremblay had made us sit through that hour-long video on the importance of expressing oneself with words rather than fists?

Well, she'd asked, and we'd deliver. "Words over fists," I said, loud enough for Ms. Tremblay to hear.

Chris smiled that same sarcastic grin I'd seen three nights before when he'd told me about how he'd hacked into his high school's computer system to change the grades of a few under-performing members of his baseball team. For a not-so-small fee, of course. I shook my head and settled back into my seat, quite sure this was going to be the most fun I'd had since being hauled into this place.

"There's more than one way to skin a cat," Chris said. "And in all that material you made us read our first day here, I didn't see anything forbidding me from owning a crossbow."

"Or an axe, for that matter," I piped up.

"Good thinking, roomie. I mean, just think about all the damage I could do with an axe. But you know what I was wondering, seeing that Ms. Tremblay assured us we were free to speak our minds and all?"

"No, what?" I asked, playing along.

"I was wondering about BB guns." Chris paused and slowly turned his head toward the security guard as if seeking his opinion. "Can I own a BB gun? Because there's this pesky raccoon that keeps tipping over the garbage cans on my street, and I'd sure like to take a shot at him every once in a while."

"That's a good question," I replied, looking to Ms. Tremblay for an answer. "The way I see it, Chris would be doing the neighborhood a favor."

"Not to mention the environment. Plus—"

"Are you two done?" Ms. Tremblay interrupted, smoothing out a non-existent wrinkle in her skirt.

"Not even close," I spit out. "You've put us through how many tests? The least we can do is have a little fun with this one."

"Is that what you think this is? Another test?"

"That's exactly what this is." I'd be stupid to think otherwise. Everything in the Bake Shop—this group session included—was designed to push us past our breaking point.

Ms. Tremblay leaned forward, her gaze fixing on me. "I

assure you, Lucas, this isn't a test. Look around—do you see any cameras?"

I did as she asked and searched the corners of the room, the ceiling, even under my chair for some sort of recording device. There was a red emergency call button next to the door, but other than that, the room looked clean.

"This truly is a chance to talk about any fears or concerns you have about returning home, Lucas."

I shook my head. She may have sounded genuine, but that didn't matter. Ms. Tremblay worked for them. "I still don't trust you," I said. "And if the rest of these guys are half as smart as me, they'll do the same and tell you nothing."

She waved the guard over, and I stood up, fully willing to leave on my own. He reached out and grabbed me, his hand circling my upper arm as he spun me around to face the wall.

Out of the corner of my eye, I saw Chris move to get up. I shook my head, motioning him to back off. There was no need for both of us to suffer because of my big mouth. Chris ignored me and took a step in my direction, his stride slow and determined, his hands balled into fists at his sides. Idiot was going to throw a punch and risk any chance he had at freedom, all to help me.

"No," I yelled as I tried to jerk free of the guard's hold. But he dug his hip into my back, warning for me to stay still. He kept one hand pressed up against the back of my head, holding me in place; the other he slammed into Chris's chest, forcefully telling him to back off.

"Let me go, I'm—"

My words were cut off by the low drone of the emergency

siren sounding in the hall. The security guard yanked me around by my shirt and grunted for me to sit before he pressed the tiny receiver lodged in his ear. His response to whatever he heard was curt; nothing more than a coded sequence of numbers and letters that had Ms. Tremblay jumping out of her chair and moving toward the door.

"Everyone up," she called out. "You know how this works. Everyone back to their rooms."

The lights flickered as she opened the door to the hall-way, the wail of the siren cutting off abruptly as if someone had purposefully disengaged the alarm.

"What's going on?" I asked Chris.

"No clue," he said. "Probably a fight in another wing or something."

I shook my head. The halls were too quiet, too empty for that. The only fight I'd witnessed so far was insane, every guard in the facility barreling down the halls and screaming orders into their comlinks. This looked different. Felt different.

I turned and sought out the guard who'd been assigned to our group session—Murphy. He didn't look too concerned; his gun was tucked back in his waistband, and he was motioning for the few stragglers to hurry up.

"I don't have time for your games right now, Lucas," he said as he pointed us toward the residence wing. "I'll let what happened back there slide, but any other issues with you and we're going to have a problem."

I nodded my thanks, unsure why he was being so lax with us, and started walking down the hall. Our room was the first on the left. The electronic keypad securing our door was dark; the red light I was used to staring at silent, dead.

The guard jabbed his fingers at the numbers, swearing when he couldn't get the panel to respond. Eventually he gave up and simply yanked on the door handle. It flew open, hitting the cinderblock wall behind it with a deafening thud.

"What's up with the doors?" I asked as I stepped into my room. Everything in this building was electronic, from the doors to our rooms to the fences surrounding the facility to the timers in the showers. We always needed a key code to enter our room—a combination that changed daily and only the security staff knew.

"Storm outside," the guard replied, as if I was an idiot for not realizing it. Right. Like I was supposed to know that. I was housed in a building with no windows, and yet I was somehow supposed to know the weather.

"And?" I asked, not sure what a little bit of wind and rain had to do with the sudden need to lock down the facility.

"Small issue with the power," Murphy explained. "The backup generators will kick in shortly, but until then, everyone is to remain in their rooms." He motioned for me to step farther into my room and reached for the door. "I wouldn't try anything. The electronic locks on the doors might not work, but you can rest assured that my Taser does."

FOUR

I woke up the next morning feeling better than ever. Sure, the power was still out and we'd spent the last twenty-five hours confined to our room, amusing ourselves with a tic-tac-toe board we carved into our floor, but the power outage had disabled the sirens and the flashing light above my bunk, affording me ten solid hours of sleep. The few lights with battery backup flickered every couple of minutes, but the surveillance camera never came back on and the electronic locks on our door never reengaged.

On top of everything, they'd decided to move us to the reintegration facility today, an entire two weeks early. At least that was something.

Stepping through the large steel front door of the Bake Shop, I stared up at the electric fence that surrounded the perimeter of the facility. It was two rows deep and capped with razor wire. Watchtowers anchored each corner, and I suspected the guards posted up there were carrying something more lethal than Taser guns.

The ground was covered in several inches of snow, and the wind whipped through the tight corridor housing the IGT van. I turned my face directly into the icy blast, catching an eyeful of snow. A month earlier, I would've despised the cold weather; I lived for summer, when my only concern was whether I had enough gas in my old Bronco to get to Narragansett Beach. Not anymore. The bitter cold slapping at my face reminded me I was almost free, no longer confined to four cement walls and a communal shower.

A guard I didn't recognize snapped his fingers in my direction, motioning for me to hurry up. *Phase 2.* We were about to enter Phase 2, reintegration. To me, that was code for *you managed to survive our tests without going batshit crazy so we're going to let you go. On our terms. In a couple of weeks. After we've made damn sure you aren't latently psychotic.*

Pass Phase 2 without incident, and we'd be shipped home with the government's "low risk" stamp of approval. And an ankle bracelet. If we could make it a year without screwing up, then we got to trade the bracelet in for the less invasive, equally humiliating scarlet letter of registering as an MAOA-L carrier. Being formally registered would earn us the opportunity to have our names distributed, confidentially of course, to the law enforcement officials in our area. Oh, and then there were the monthly meetings with a program-appointed shrink.

The latently psychotic stuff, I got. It's not like the effects of sleep deprivation took hold the first night. Everything they'd subjected us to was gradual, designed to steadily chip away at our self-control until we cracked. But I didn't care about any of that; it was all the other baggage that came along with going home that pissed me off.

The side door to the van was already open, four of the guys in our group settling into the back seats. I climbed the two steps and inched my way across the middle seat, seeking out a window.

"Damn, it's cold out here," Chris grumbled as he took the seat next to me. "Why the hell would they move us now? I mean, look at it out there. It's a blizzard."

I shrugged. Sure, it was snowing, but I'd seen worse. Plus, I wasn't about to complain.

"Think it has anything to do with the power still being out?" Chris asked.

"Probably," I said, remembering the lights dimming as we made our way down the exit corridor to the van. "I heard the guards talking when they brought us our breakfast this morning. There's a new group coming in today. Without the electronic safety measures powered up, I guess they figure they need the guards assigned to us to cover the newbies."

"And what? We're the safest ones to move out, so we get the honor of freezing our asses off in the van so they can keep their little impound schedule intact?"

"Seems so," I replied.

Chris laughed, his amusement drawing the attention of everyone in the van. "Who would've thought a place like this, a place designed to test less than one percent of the population, would have a security problem?"

"Beats me," I said.

The driver closed the door, and I took a quick head

count. Ten of us, a driver, and a guard, all shoved into this nasty-smelling van, grunting as we tried to find a comfortable position. Short, tall, fat, thin; there was nothing physically binding the ten of us together, except maybe our exhaustion. And that damn gene.

I blew a puff of air onto the window and watched as the fog vanished, leaving behind traces of liquid. It was pathetic, really. I'd spent the last two years of my life purposefully staying out of trouble, not wanting to give anybody a reason to suspect that I carried the gene. But I ended up here anyway. Thinking back on it, I should've made the time worthy of the punishment, maybe put a few rocks through the windows at school or practiced my batting swing on the neighbors' mailboxes.

I shook off that useless string of *what ifs* and stared down at my feet. They were cold. The floor vents in the van apparently didn't work, and I curled my toes into my shoes, the tiny movement making me wince. Damn sneakers were half a size too small, and my feet had been aching since day one.

I reached down to untie them, my hand grazing across a piece of paper stuck to the metal frame of the seat in front of me. Bored and curious, I tore it free, ripping it in the process.

"What's that?" Chris asked, and I held up the pamphlet for him to see. He cocked his head and recited the text: "*A coed testing facility for adolescents, providing a supportive and nurturing environment committed to ensuring every individual leads a safe, happy, and productive life.*"

"Must've been left over from the last group they brought in," I said. "I wonder if any of them believed a word of it."

"Hope not. And that coed part is a crock of shit. I haven't

run across a single girl in this place. Unless you count Ms. Tremblay. Which I don't," he quickly clarified. "And God knows a few girls would've at least made my time there a little more interesting."

I laughed. Leave it to Chris to ignore the "supportive and nurturing environment" crap and hone in on the word "coed." But my smile slipped away as I considered his words more carefully. I hadn't seen any girls in there either, and for a whole host of messed-up reasons, I was glad.

"Doubt a girl would survive their tests," I said, picturing a grown-up version of Suzie trapped inside the Bake Shop.

I knew that the chances of her—of any girl—testing positive for the gene were one in a million, but that didn't stop the terror from worming its way though my core. My mind conjured up images of her secluded in a dark room for hours as they watched her through a two-way mirror, waiting to see if the loneliness gave way to something darker. Even I had cursed the fear that wove through my system during that test, my tears collecting in the hollow of my neck as I begged for someone to talk to me, hit me, do anything so I'd know I wasn't alone. And I knew what to expect—knew from Tyler's journal that that particular torment only lasted six hours.

"No, a girl probably wouldn't," Chris replied. "You think … I mean, if there was a girl in there, you think they'd go easier on her?"

I didn't miss the hesitation in Chris's voice or the fear that accompanied his question. He didn't have any sisters, but that didn't mean he didn't have a cousin or a girlfriend. Didn't mean it wasn't their face he was envisioning.

"Can I have it?" he added.

"Have what?"

"The brochure."

"Sure," I said, tossing it his direction, not caring whether or not I ever saw the damn thing again. They could keep their glossy pictures and well-crafted lies. My memories of that place were all I needed.

FIVE

The inside of the van smelled nasty and my ears were clogged, the pressure building to a nearly intolerable level as we made our slow descent down the mountain. I'd have given anything for my iPod, a pack of gum, a bottle of water ... anything to make my ears pop.

I pulled the hood of my sweatshirt tighter around my head and changed positions. The van's seats were rock-hard, and the guy in the row behind me kept jabbing his foot into my back. But no matter what I did, no matter what angle I twisted my body into, I couldn't get comfortable.

Every few minutes, I'd catch Chris staring at one of the guys, his gaze narrowing as if he was trying to figure them out. I'd done the same thing myself; and, if any of us were going to have a delayed reaction to the testing, my money was on the scrawny kid directly in front of us. From the smell pouring off him and the rather greasy tinge to his hair, my guess was he hadn't showered since his first day at the Bake Shop. To make things worse, he was muttering to himself, so much so that the guard in the back of the van had angled his body to better watch him.

I yanked on the seat belt digging into my shoulder, half considering taking it off. But the roads were slick, and that narrow strap of nylon had saved me from sliding sideways into Chris's lap more than a couple of times already.

"You nervous?" I asked Chris. He may have been lazily watching the passing trees, but his leg was bouncing a mile a minute, shaking the entire seat.

"Nope," he replied, never taking his eyes off the road. "I figure it can't be any worse than what we've already been through."

He wasn't looking for an answer, but I nodded anyway. He was right. The tests were one thing, but it was the sensation of constantly being watched that had me struggling to stay sane. If the reintegration facility was less intense, if people weren't constantly tracking my every move, then maybe I could survive this nightmare after all.

"According to the brochure, they even have a gaming system there," Chris continued.

"I wouldn't hold your breath on that one," I said. None of Tyler's journal entries had mentioned a gaming system, and the one thing he'd loved nearly as much as his girlfriend was shooting virtual zombies. I snagged the brochure from underneath Chris's leg and flipped through the pages. Sure enough, there was a picture of a gaming system and a flat-screen TV. For some reason, I suspected that was a picture of a staff lounge and not our communal meeting room.

"You got a girlfriend back home?" I asked Chris. I'd

avoided asking him any personal questions up to this point. But I was bored out of my mind and a tiny bit curious.

Chris shook his head but stayed silent.

"Me either," I replied. "Once Tyler tested positive, I pretty much became every parent's worst nightmare. Being labeled potentially psychotic doesn't exactly make you prime dating material."

Chris turned at my words, no doubt surprised I was volunteering to talk about anything personal. "What really happened with your brother?" he asked.

"They broke him," I breathed out. "He was with the first group that got tested. They took him a little over two years ago. Same testing facility, same series of tests."

There were only six of them at the Bake Shop then. They'd kept three of the guys for further evaluation, and three they'd sent home. I'd looked up the other two after Tyler died. I wanted to see how they were doing, if they were as messed-up as my brother. They were alive, but neither of them was still in school. Neither of them had a job. As far as I could tell, they were barely existing.

"What was he like when he came home?" Chris asked.

"Different," I replied. "Angry. Closed off. Isolated. Take your pick."

"What about his friends? His girlfriend? Yesterday, back at that stupid therapy session, you said everybody would turn on us once we got home. Did they turn on him?" Chris asked, and I couldn't help but wonder if that was his biggest fear. Not failing these tests. Not have to register as a MAOA-L carrier. Rather, that the people he'd grown to love would all reject him.

I smiled as I recalled Olivia. She was one person who'd never turned her back on Tyler, the only one who could get him to talk. "His girlfriend didn't turn on him. Neither did his best friend, Nick. Olivia was waiting for Tyler the day he got home." *She's with him now*, I silently added.

"So then you knew," Chis said, a few minutes later. "I mean, you knew that if your brother tested positive, chances were you would too."

"Yup." I'd known my days were numbered when Sheriff Watts first showed up for Tyler. The fact that I'd also tested positive wasn't coincidental. The gene was hereditary, passed from one generation to the next.

"So why didn't you run?" Chris asked. "Why didn't you take off the day before your seventeenth birthday?"

"I thought about it." I'd actually done more than just think about it—I'd completely mapped it out, had even started stashing supplies in the shed behind our house. Plan was to toss all my belongings into my Bronco and head for the Canadian border, but I didn't have a passport or any real money to speak of. Plus, in my mind, running was like letting them win, admitting that I was scared of failing their tests. And scared or not, I wasn't about to let them win.

"I had nowhere to go," I finally admitted. "It's not like anyone was going to help me. Most of our friends wanted nothing to do with me after Tyler, and it's not like people are overly excited to help a teenager with sociopath potential. So I figured, why put off the inevitable. Why let them see my fear and win?"

"They won't break us." There was an edge of defiance in Chris's tone, one that had me chuckling. He was as determined as I was to prove Ms. Tremblay and every last guard in that place wrong. To prove to the world that we weren't hardwired to kill.

"I would have run," Chris mumbled under his breath.

I couldn't say I blamed him. Looking back on it, I probably should have.

SIX

I'd forgotten how long it could take to go forty miles on snow-covered roads, let alone in an oversized, top-heavy van. What should've been a quick one-hour drive was painfully dragging on, the boredom of the trip bordering on psychological torture. I closed my eyes and leaned my head against the window. How the other guys in the van had managed to fall asleep was beyond me. Every few minutes, we'd hit a bump in the road and my head would bounce off the glass, painfully jarring me awake.

"What time is it?" Chris asked as he stretched beside me. He hadn't been able to sleep either and had taken to picking at the small tear in the vinyl seat between us. There was a gaping hole there now, a wad of yellowish foam scattered by his feet.

"No clue," I said. I'd given up trying to guess the time and started tracking our progress by counting the number of moose-crossing signs we passed. Only two in the last hour. "Probably late afternoon."

"This is insane. We could walk there faster," Chris moaned.

He was right. At this rate, it'd be morning before we got to the reintegration facility. Sure, it was snowing when we left, but things had gotten noticeably worse in the last hour. The lines marking the sides of the road were no longer visible; only a guardrail marked our route. That was it. No cement blocks, no breakdown lane, just a waist-high strip of metal designed to keep us from literally falling off the side of the mountain.

The road narrowed, and our van slowed to a near stop as the driver navigated his way around a downed tree. I questioned why he just didn't pull over and move it. It was a scrawny pitch pine no more than a few inches thick. Any one of us could've shoved it out of the way, the driver and security guard included. And given how desperate I was to piss, I would've gladly volunteered.

"Idiots," the driver mumbled as he eased the van around a second fallen tree, barely clearing it. "I deserve hazard pay for this."

His eyes darted to the window on his left, then back to the road before he used the rear-view mirror to signal the security guard behind us. Chris saw it too and craned his neck to catch the guard's response.

"What?" I mouthed to Chris.

"Something's not right. The guard in the back is acting weird, and the driver is going way too slow."

"Crappy roads," I offered up. With the wind whipping the snow around, there were times you couldn't see more than three feet in front of you.

"Nah, that's not it," Chris said. "The roads are bad, but

the van is heavy. Besides, it seems the driver is more focused on the woods than on the road."

We slowed to a crawl again, a third, larger tree encroaching on our lane. I leaned over the seat in front of me and peered out the windshield, focusing on the dark shadows looming ahead. The road had leveled off and the wind had momentarily stopped, giving me a clear view of what lay ahead. It took a few seconds, but I made out the shapes of several more downed trees. One on the right side of the road, the other on the left. It continued like that for as far as I could see, like a zigzag pattern forcing the driver to literally weave his way down the already narrow road.

I flashed another concerned look at Chris. It was definitely windy enough for the storm to have knocked over some trees, but why like that? Why in such a weird pattern? And why so close to each other?

The guard in the back row swung his head around to look at the tree we'd just passed. I'd bet my life we were thinking the same thing. The fallen trees were perfectly spaced, each one coming closer and closer to completely blocking the road. Like someone had purposefully dropped them that way. Like someone was trying to slow us down.

Not wanting to draw attention to myself, I kicked Chris's foot and tilted my head toward the window. "Trees. All down," I whispered.

Chris looked at me like I was insane—the same way everybody at school had looked at me when they found out my brother tested positive. But I wasn't crazy then, and I sure as hell wasn't crazy now. "Just look. No way the trees fell on their own like that."

A muffled curse drew my attention forward. The driver's hands were wrapped around the steering wheel, his knuckles white, his eyes darting in a frantic pattern from the windshield to the passenger-side window. He muttered something under his breath, then leaned over and keyed in a code on the small lockbox resting on the center console.

"Gun," Chris said, his eyes no longer trained on the woods outside but on the guard in the back seat. The guard was fumbling with a lockbox of his own, his hands shaking so hard that it took him three tries to key in the right code.

"Shit, those aren't Tasers," I said as the driver jammed the clip into place and released the safety. I took one quick look around the van. No one had moved. No one had so much as sneezed.

"Who?" I asked, completely confused as to where the threat was coming from. There were no tire tracks on the opposite side of the road, no masked men waving guns or demanding that we pull over.

I cupped my hands around my eyes and leaned into the window, my vision honing in on the woods slowly creeping by. "Nothing. There's nothing out there."

A glint of light caught my attention, and I leaned forward, shoving the guy in the seat in front of me aside so I had a clear view of the road. My pulse quickened, my hands clawing into the seat as I screamed at Chris to hang on. We had three seconds—five at most—to brace ourselves before we hit the van barreling toward us.

SEVEN

The entire world slowed down, every fiber of my being hyper-focusing on the chaos unfolding. Every smell, every sound, every broken cry echoed around me in unimaginable clarity.

Our driver pounded his foot on the brake, but it was too late. We were skating all over the road, the snow-covered pavement slick and uncooperative. The driver had two options: he could steer us away from the oncoming van and into the guardrail, or hit the other vehicle head-on.

Our van's brakes locked up, the high-pitched squeal reverberating through the van. Our driver yanked on the emergency brake, probably hoping to slow our momentum, but all that did was jam up the rear wheels, causing us to slide even more. We picked up speed, the backside of the van fishtailing, violently swinging us back and forth.

The security guard in the back seat swore long and hard, then yelled at us to brace ourselves. The silence that followed was short and deafening, each one of us staring straight ahead. Watching. Waiting.

The van lurched to the right, and I braced my feet against the metal frame of the seat in front of me as I prayed to whatever God was listening to let me live. Screams erupted seconds before we slammed into the other van. I pushed those panicked sounds to the back of my mind, my senses completely overtaken by the feel of the tires struggling to gain traction and the smell of fresh-cut pine and piss. All of them mingled together into one terrifying moment.

The force of the collision tossed me backward. The van tipped, steadying itself at a perilous angle before slamming down onto the guardrail. It landed on its side, tearing through the metal. Through all the noise, I heard a thump—the unmistakable sound of someone's head hitting the side of the van—immediately followed by a sickly warm spray of blood coating my seat. Coating me.

The van slid downhill, a blur of shrieking metal and sparks igniting the air as we bounced from boulder to boulder. The snow did nothing to slow our descent, and we plowed into a tree, then rolled two times before jolting to a stop.

Strangled breaths replaced the chaos, the sound too quiet to be comforting. Afraid that the slightest motion would set us tumbling again, I didn't move. I didn't even dare to blink. I simply lay there, listening to the unsettling silence.

Tentatively, I stretched out my legs, then my arms, breathing a sigh of relieve at the sheer agony the movement brought. If I was in pain, then I was alive.

I swept my hand out to my right, searching for Chris. My fingers landed on something solid and wet. I reluctantly turned my head, seeking him out.

"Chris?" I had to swallow twice to get that one word out. Even then, it was rough, the ragged sound sputtering from my chest in a strangled whisper. Chris didn't answer, and I tugged at the seat belt digging into my shoulder, desperate to get free so I could see if he was alive.

A thin streak of blood trailed down the left side of his face, his hair was covered in pine needles and chunks of glass, and his shirt was soaked with what looked like vomit. "Chris, answer me!" I yelled as I wrapped my hands around his upper arms and began shaking him. There was no way he could be dead. There was no way I would allow him to be dead.

His breath came out in a hard gasp, his entire body shuddering with the effort. He opened his eyes, his gaze locking on some point in the distance. I let him sit like that until the haze lifted and the realization of what had happened finally set in.

"Lucas?" My name was choked, cut off by what I thought was fear.

I swiped my eyes, embarrassed by my tears, and smiled. "Yep, it's me. You okay?"

"Hell no," Chris said as he struggled to find the latch of his seat belt. I went to help, but he shoved my hands aside, determined to do it himself. "Do I look okay?"

I looked around the van, horror quickly replacing my relief. No one was in the seat they'd started in. Their bodies had been tossed around, landing in grotesque, unnatural positions. We'd all been told to buckle up when we first left the facility, but an hour into the trip, even the security guard had taken his seat belt off in an effort get more comfortable. Whatever had possessed Chris and me to leave ours on was beyond me.

A soft groan caught my attention, and I looked back at Chis. He was staggering to his feet, one hand firmly planted over the gash on his side of his head. "I need to get out of here." The hand he was pressing to his wound moved to cover his mouth. "I'm gonna puke."

Miraculously, our van had landed upright, but the doors were caved in. The only way out was over several limp bodies and through the shattered windshield. "That way," I said, pointing toward the front.

No matter where I put my foot or my hand, it always seemed to land on a person. Or some part of a person. Eventually I gave up being careful and purposefully started planting my palms on their bloodied chests, hoping to get them to scream, to cough, to give me some indication that they were alive. I would've pulled every one of them out. I swear I would've, had any of them so much as moaned.

"We can't leave them," Chris said as he placed two fingers on the side of someone's neck. "Some of them might still be alive."

"They're not," I said, slamming my foot into the windshield and kicking out the remains of the shattered glass. I needed to get out this van, away from the dead bodies lying around me and the overwhelming fear threatening to paralyze me in place.

I stumbled out into the snow and fell to my knees. Chris crawled out behind me, then collapsed to the ground beside me. I lay there for a second watching the blood drip from his head, staining the snow in an odd polka-dot pattern.

"You messed up your head," I finally said, pointing to the cut above his right eye. It was still bleeding and caked with dirt, probably deep enough to need stitches.

He swiped his hand across his forehead, wincing. "Wouldn't be the first time," he replied as he stared down at his blood-coated fingers. "What do we do now?"

"Nothing," I said, completely content to lie there and let the snow numb my entire body.

"We're alive," Chris choked out a few minutes later. "We're actually alive."

I mumbled a weak "yes" and continued watching his blood trickle onto the snow. The bleeding had slowed enough that I could count to ten before the next drop fell. A speck of gray dropped into the pool of blood, and I stared at it for a minute, trying to figure out what it was. A second, marble-sized rock fell next to it, and I jerked my head toward the road, panic screaming through my body.

The stones falling toward us were getting bigger; the last one hit me in the chest, stealing my breath. The sound of metal whining in protest drifted through the air, and I looked up, following the path of the falling rocks. The other van was directly above us, its back tires caught on what was left of the guardrail.

"We've got to get out of here." I rolled over and pushed myself upright. The debris was tumbling down the embankment even faster, pinging off boulders and trees before settling on the ground around us. We had minutes, maybe only seconds, before the other van lost its balance and came skidding down the cliff, crushing us.

"Give me a second," Chris said. He pushed himself up off the ground and climbed back through the van's broken windshield.

"Are you crazy?" I yelled, pointing toward the wall of rock sliding toward us. "We don't have time to pull anybody out."

"I'm not planning on it," Chris said, poking at our driver with his foot. The man didn't move, didn't so much as grunt. Chris rolled him over, gagging at the sight of his mangled face. Swallowing hard, he dug his hand into the man's pocket and pulled out his phone. The screen was nothing more than a giant spider web of cracks, but Chris hit the power button anyway, muttering a prayer that it would work. He got nothing, not even a dim flicker of light.

"Check the ground. The guard must've had a phone too," Chris said as he tossed the broken one aside.

I had no desire to crawl back into that wreckage, to cement those mangled bodies in my memory as I searched for a phone I knew wouldn't work. But I quickly looked around anyway, hoping to find a perfectly intact and functioning phone just lying there in the snow.

"There's no way we're going to get a signal out here," I said as another wave of rocks skidded down the hill, landing inches from where I stood. "Forget about a phone. We gotta move. Now!"

I stumbled over my own feet, fighting the shakiness in my legs as I attempted to navigate the uneven ground quickly. Stopping a few feet away, I slowed down to wait for Chris, my attention completely focused on the steady flow of rocks tumbling toward us.

We carefully picked our way up the rocky bank. For every three steps we took, we slid back two, adding more bruises to our already battered bodies. The van above us was swaying, and I shifted my course, losing ground but steering clear of the van's eventual downward path.

I cleared the last boulder, was only steps from the road, when I waved Chris to a stop. "You hear that?" I asked. I was positive I'd heard something—like a knocking, only deeper. The knocking turned to a scream, and I heaved myself up and over the guardrail, then took off running for the van.

It was identical to ours, the letters IGT decaled on the driver's-side door. They'd been headed to the Bake Shop. That van was full of guys just like us—the newbies from the intake facility. The ones we'd been moved out to make room for.

"It's gonna go," Chris called after me. "There's no way you're going to make it in time."

I would. I just needed to stay on my feet, to push my pain aside and will my body to move.

The van lurched, the guardrail pulling free of its anchors with a thunderous pop before the vehicle rolled forward. A hand flattened against the inside of the window as the van began to slide over the bank, the terrified eyes of the people trapped inside pleading with me for help.

I collapsed on the snow-covered road and screamed out my rage as the van disappeared over the side of the cliff. It didn't roll like ours. It plummeted straight down, smashing into our van and exploding in a ball of fiery red.

"They were alive," I choked out, cursing myself for not making it to them sooner, for wasting precious seconds resting in the snow rather than racing up to help them. "They were alive."

"We tried," Chris said, falling to his knees beside me.

I shook my head, my world spinning violently with the motion. The fact that I'd tried wasn't good enough for me. All that mattered was that I'd failed.

Glenrock Branch Library
Box 1000
Glenrock, WY 82637

EIGHT

The pain I'd been pushing aside crashed into me with a vengeance. I coughed, ignoring the tinge of blood I could taste circling my mouth, and focused instead on the burning pinpricks biting at my legs.

The road was littered with glass and shards of metal, and I was kneeling in it, had been for the last ten minutes. I forced myself to stand and searched for a clean spot to rest. But no matter where I looked, all I saw was dirty snow littered with debris. Debris and the occasional splatter of blood.

"You going to be all right?" Chris asked.

I shook my head, unable to grab on to a single one of the thousand thoughts flying through my brain. Everything hurt and nothing made sense. In the end, the only thing that struck me with any clarity was the image of a guy's hand pressing against the window of that van and my inability to help him.

I tried to heave myself off the ground, but my body protested, an impressive array of dark spots clouding my vision. I finally gave up and slumped back to the road, content to just die right there.

Chris sat down next to me and began poking at a hole in his jeans like he was trying to wedge something free. It wasn't until I heard the clink of glass bouncing off what was left of the guardrail that I realized what he was doing—pulling a large shard of glass out of his leg.

"You made it all the way up here with that thing stuck in you?" I asked, amazed at his tolerance for pain.

"Nope. I'm pretty sure I got it *on* the way up here."

I looked down at my own pants. They were torn in several places, dirt and tiny pieces of glass stuck in the fabric. But I wasn't bleeding, not as bad as Chris anyway.

"Any ideas?" I asked. The road was deserted, only one set of tracks coming in each direction, and even those were beginning to disappear under the still-falling snow.

"Start walking, I guess," Chris said. "Sitting here isn't exactly an option. It's not like we passed a crapload of gas stations or 7-Elevens."

He was right. My toes were already numb and most of my body ached. Plus, sitting here, staring at the charred remains of the vans down below, wasn't something I wanted to do. I'd walk as far as I could until either my body or daylight gave out.

"Sounds like a plan," I said, struggling to my feet.

"Any idea which way we came from?" Chris asked.

"That way, I think," I said, turning a complete circle in the road. "The guardrail was on our right, which means we were coming from that way."

Less than a quarter-mile down the road, Chris stopped walking and bent over, trying to catch his breath. He was hurt but fighting it. I wasn't in much better shape. My lungs burned, my ribs ached, and the throbbing in my shoulder was getting worse. Between the pain and the cold that had lodged itself in my bones, I wasn't going to make it much farther myself.

We spotted a break in the road up ahead, a small path that looked like it led into the woods. "Think we should stop for a while and wait the storm out?" I asked, pointing to the path.

"Nope, I'm fine," Chris replied as he straightened up. "I just need a minute to rest."

I doubted a minute was going to make that much of a difference. What we needed was to find a place where we could sit down for a few hours, a place where the wind wasn't constantly lashing at our backs. "This road is like one giant wind tunnel," I said as I dug my hands deeper into the pockets of my sweatshirt. "It would be warmer in the woods."

"If we leave the road, the chances of us being found are slim to none, and I didn't crawl my way out of that van only to freeze to death in the woods," Chris said.

"Being found may be the last thing we want," I replied. We'd survived an accident that had killed everybody else in our van, it was butt-ass cold and snowing, and we hadn't passed a car, a search party, or even so much as a dead animal since we'd climbed back up the side of that mountain. Hiking back to the testing facility was one thing—I knew the guards there, could gauge their reactions and adjust mine in turn. It was people out hunting deer or trapping foxes that I didn't want to run into. Most people considered us dangerous, and . . . well, they'd have rifles to back up their prejudice.

"Trust me, there's nobody out here worth running into," I went on. "I say we find a hole and crawl into it, wait out the storm, and hike back to the Bake Shop tomorrow morning."

NINE

We ended up taking shelter on the side of the road, hidden behind the trees but still close enough to see the road. The sky had cleared, bringing with it a searing cold. I huddled into myself and closed my eyes, never once contemplating sleep. Since I was dressed only in a sweatshirt and jeans, sleep was my enemy. Had I given in to my exhaustion, I might very well have frozen to death.

Looking for something to keep my mind alert, I started listening to the sounds around me, isolating each one. A screech owl in the distance calling out to his mate. The gentle howl of the wind as it tore through the tops of the pitch pines. The crunching of snow underfoot.

The crunching of snow underfoot?

That last sound had my eyes flashing wide, and I scanned the area as my mind cycled through a crapload of disturbing possibilities.

Chris had heard it too, his gaze lost in the dark tangle of trees surrounding us. "There," he said, pointing to an outcropping of rocks in the distance. "Person."

It took me a second to see the person; the faded jeans and dirty gray jacket blended perfectly with the wall of rock behind them. It wasn't until they finally broke the stillness by standing up that I finally realized who it was.

A girl. And from the looks of it, she was scared shitless. Of me.

I held up my hands, hoping she'd realize I was unarmed and had no intention of harming her. Her eyes trailed to Chris, and she took a tiny step backward as if somehow she perceived him to be the bigger threat.

"He won't hurt you either," I said as I stood up and took a tentative step toward her.

Chris stood up too, his eyes now furiously scanning the area for others. He went to speak, but I held up my hand for him to stop. The girl was clearly spooked, and I doubted us crowding her space was going to help.

"Are you hurt?" I asked. From what I could see, she looked relatively unharmed. Her knuckles were bloody, her coat was torn, and her hair was a mess of dirt and pine needles. I didn't see any gaping wounds or insane amounts of blood. But she was alone. In the woods. At night. And as far as I knew, there was never a good reason for that.

"I'm Lucas, and this is Chris," I said, motioning for Chris to stop moving. He'd been taking tiny steps towards her the entire time, forcing her farther from the outcropping of rocks she'd been hiding behind and out into the open road.

"What's your name?" I asked.

"Carly." It came out barely as a whisper. "Carly Denton."

Tyler's face suddenly flashed across my mind, the image

of his girlfriend's quickly following on its heels. *Denton?* Tyler's girlfriend's name was Olivia. Olivia Denton.

I closed the space between us in four giant steps. I hadn't seen the resemblance at first, but up this close, it was undeniable. Her hair was the same auburn color as Olivia's, and her eyes … they were the exact same shade of ice blue. And they were every bit as sad.

I hadn't seen Olivia since the day we buried my brother. I'd gone back to Tyler's grave later that night to say goodbye to him in private. Olivia was sitting there, her hands sunk deep into the dirt, talking to Tyler as if he were sitting right there next to her. I didn't expect her to do what she did; I thought her parting words of "I'll see you soon" were nothing more than a promise to visit his grave the next day. If I'd known, if I'd only taken the time to stop by her house on my way home, maybe she'd still be here.

"I know you," I said. "You're Olivia's sister."

She nodded and backed away, her eyes flickering to Chris. I saw the request in them, the silent plea for me to protect her from him. It split me in two. "He won't hurt you," I said again. "Neither of us will."

She ignored me, her eyes darting to the trees surrounding us, looking for the quickest way to escape.

"Do you know who I am?" I asked. "Do you recognize me at all?"

"No," she said.

It made sense, I guess. We'd never actually been formally introduced. She was a year younger than me and went to a different school. The only time we'd been within touching distance of each other was at Tyler's funeral, and needless to say, I hadn't been paying much attention to who was there.

"I'm Lucas," I said, hoping the sound of my name would jar her memory. "Lucas Marshall. Tyler's brother."

———————

We stood like that forever—Carly's eyes darting from my hair, to my mouth, to the hole in my jeans—while Chris watched from a distance, confused.

"Umm, I take it you two know each other?" Chris said.

I nodded and Carly remained silent. She looked nervous, her weight shifting from one leg to the other as she scanned the tree line. I didn't know what, or rather who, she was looking for, but it was obvious she didn't feel safe out in the open. With us.

"Yeah, we know each other. Well, we know of each other. Carly, meet Chris; Chris, meet Carly," I said, waving my hands between the two of them.

"And how, exactly, do you know her?" Chris seemed skeptical. I couldn't blame him. It was one thing to run into people you knew at the movies, or the mall, or the grocery store. But out in the middle of nowhere in the wake of a blizzard? Yeah, that was weird.

"Her last name is Denton," I said, answering Chris's question. "She's from my hometown. Her sister used to date my brother." I turned back to Carly. "What are you doing here?"

"What am I doing here?" she asked, reiterating my question. "Why are you here? You're supposed to be locked up inside."

Her gaze shifted to the tangle of trees behind us, and she started taking tiny steps backward again. Her hands tensed at her sides and she turned slightly, her stance widening as if she were getting ready to run.

"Come here," I said softly, coaxing her forward. For the life of me, I couldn't understand why she was so scared of me.

"You screw her over or something back home?" Chris asked as he watched Carly hold her ground, her feet melding to the snow-covered road. "Because that girl looks more than a little freaked to see you."

"Shut the hell up," I yelled. I hadn't merely screwed Carly over, I'd let her only sister die. I'd been so fixated on my own grief that I'd ignored every word Olivia uttered at my brother's grave.

"I'm not scared of you," she quickly spit out. "You're Lucas? You're Tyler's brother? And you're really here, standing in front of me?"

I nodded, a small smile creeping across my face. Even out here, in the midst of an epically screwed-up situation, it was nice to see someone from home. Nice to know that there was a least one person who was actually happy I was still around. "Yep. Why, were you looking for me?"

"Were you on that van?" she asked. "The one I saw go over the cliff and explode?"

Chris shot me a look, one I immediately recognized. Suspicion. He didn't trust her, and no amount of history between us was going to change that.

"Nope," he said to her. "We were in the van that hit it. We got the honor of clawing our way out through the windshield and freezing our asses off as we hiked God knows how many miles back."

"Wait—you're walking back to the testing facility? After everything they did to you, you're actually heading back there? Willingly?"

"That was the plan," Chris snapped.

"Take me with you." Carly clamped her hand around my wrist, refusing to let go, pleading with me not to leave her alone on the road. "Please, Lucas, take me back there with you."

"Umm … yeah, no," Chris answered for me. "Trust me, that's the last place you want to go."

"That's exactly where I need to go," she said and started walking that direction, dragging me along beside her.

TEN

"Stop," I yelled, yanking back on her hold. Chris and I had hunkered down on the side of the road for a reason—because neither of us had the strength to move at the moment. And Carly showing up hadn't changed that.

"Not yet," I added, pointing toward the small clearing we'd taken shelter in earlier. It wasn't an ideal spot, but the sweeping tree branches at least offered some shelter from the blowing snow. "Chris wasn't lying. We literally just climbed out of a car wreck. Can you at least give us a few minutes to regroup?"

Chris mumbled something about letting her find her own way back, but I ignored him and settled onto the frozen ground. Carly took a seat across from me, her eyes softening as she took in Chris's injuries. I leaned my back against the tree and stretched out my legs. It felt fantastic to stop, just sit and not move. To not think for a few seconds.

I groaned at the piercing numbness settling into my toes. The trees we were hiding behind did little to muffle the sound of the howling wind. My body had given out, was aching to the point of agony, and my mind was in a bad place. The soundtrack of the crash replayed itself over and over in my mind. The memory of screeching tires and the smell of blood and vomit were enough to have me swallowing back bile all over again. I could've dealt with those images; since Tyler's death, I'd gotten pretty adept at ignoring my nightmares. But what kept my mind spinning on high gear was the girl sitting across from me and the thousand questions I had for her.

"You think he'll be okay?" Carly asked. She'd been staring at a sleeping Chris for the past ten minutes, a look of guilt marring her features.

These were the first words she'd spoken since we'd sat down, and they caught me off guard. I looked over at Chris and nodded. He was snoring like he always did, loud and full of grunts. Plus, he was the strongest person I knew, had gone through the same series of tests I had, and not once had he shown a single sign of cracking.

"He'll be fine," I said, praying I was right. "You want to tell me why you're so intent on getting to the testing facility?" The only person she knew in that place was me, and I could all but guarantee everybody from back home had written me off.

She wavered for a minute, as if debating whether to tell me the truth. "I know what happens to people in there," she finally said. "And I won't let them—"

I shook my head, nearly chuckling at the stupidity of her last statement. "You have no idea what goes on in that facility. If you did, you'd be running in the opposite direction rather than begging me to take you there."

"Not true," she said. "I know everything that goes on in there. I know what happens from the second you walk into that place until the day they drop you back home. I know they strip you of all your personal belongings. I know about the tests, and the cinderblock walls, and the cameras mounted everywhere."

"How so?" I asked, remembering my brief two-hour layover at the intake center. They'd taken every personal item they'd found on me, including my picture of Tyler. They tossed it in a Ziploc bag, then labeled it with a series of numbers. They didn't even use my last name.

"I have Tyler's notes. The ones he wrote to Olivia each day."

Chris muttered something from his spot on the ground, his eyes finally opening. "That's bullshit, and you know it. Rules haven't changed at all since he was there. No letters, no communication with the outside world at all."

"I never said he wrote them inside. He had a journal; he used to write in it at night when Olivia was asleep. Your mother gave it to my sister the day of Tyler's funeral."

An inexplicable amount of shame filled me. I knew what was in that journal, knew it outlined every test my brother had suffered through and his body's disgusting reaction to most of them. And just sitting there, watching the pity roll through her eyes, I knew what she was doing— taking everything she'd read and applying it to me.

I'd begged my mother not to give the journal to Olivia for this exact reason. I didn't want anybody to know what they'd done to Tyler, what they would eventually do to me. But mom disagreed, said they were addressed to Olivia for a reason.

"Still haven't answered his question." Chris was on his feet now, inching closer to Carly with each of his clipped words. "Why. Are. You. Here?"

She stood up, her eyes darting to me. I briefly toyed with backing Chris down, but Carly Denton had a crap-ton of secrets, all of which she was hiding from me.

"You're hiding something." Chris was within two feet of her, towering over her, demanding answers.

She inched her way backward, weaving around the thin pines. Chris matched her step for step. She misjudged her footing and slipped, her back slamming into the tree behind her.

"Chris," I yelled, stepping between them. Carly was slowly sliding to the ground, holding her hands out, silently begging him to stop. "What the hell? You're scaring the crap out of her."

I'd known Chris for only a month, but through all the tests we'd endured, he'd always remained calm, level-headed. Now he seemed barely this side of crazy. If he kept it up, Carly would never talk.

"You may have some warped sense of obligation toward this girl, Lucas, but I don't. Something's been off with her since she showed up, and I want to know what it is." He ducked his head around my shoulder, jabbing a finger in Carly's direction. "And I want her to tell me. Now!"

A flash of panic lit up Carly's eyes, and I shoved Chris back to give her some space to breath. She quickly jumped to her feet and sprinted into the woods.

"Lucas!" Chris shouted, and I took off after her. She only

made it a few feet before I hooked my arms around her waist and pulled her into my chest, holding her in place. Carly kicked out at me, her hands clawing at my arms. I squeezed tighter, a not-so-gentle demand for her to stop.

"Enough," I said, gritting my teeth. Her nails were digging into my skin, the thin weight of my sweatshirt offering little protection against her rage. "I already told you I'm not going to hurt you, and neither is Chris."

Carly's response to my promise was nothing more than a high-pitched shriek, one that had me contemplating dropping her right then so I could cover my ears. Luckily my brain kicked in, and I clamped one of my hands over her mouth, smothering her scream.

I slid to the ground with her in my arms, anchoring her to my chest.

"You scream like that again, and everybody within a hundred-mile radius of us will hear you and come running, guns pointed. You want that?" Chris asked, and she shook her head. "You ready to explain to them how all those trees fell in such a perfect order? Or maybe tell them why there are a bunch of dead teenagers down there? Because the more I sit here thinking about it, the more convinced I am that you had something to do with it."

"I'm going to let you go now," I said. "But if you think about screaming again, then I'm going to let Chris over there sit on you, got it?"

Carly nodded, and I eased up my grip. "Got it?" I asked one more time before completely letting her go.

She scampered out of my reach and dropped to the

ground a good ten feet away from me, her eyes, yet again, searching the woods.

Chris kicked at the snow-covered ground beneath his boots, staring into the dead space that Carly was so fixated on. "You've been staring into those damn woods since we found you. What the hell are you looking for?"

"Nobody."

"Interesting," Chris said as he reached down, picked up a rock, and started tossing it back and forth between his hands. "I asked you 'what,' and you come back with 'nobody.'"

Panic seized Carly's features. "It wasn't supposed to happen this way."

"What wasn't supposed to happen this way?" I asked.

"They weren't supposed to die. Nobody was supposed to get hurt. We wanted the van to stop, that's all. There was only supposed to be one van on the road, not two. A van from Intake, headed to the testing facility. I knew the day you went in, Lucas, and I knew the exact day you were supposed to be coming out. You weren't supposed to be on the road. I never would've agreed to it if I'd known there'd be more than one van. None of us would've."

She was rattling off these vague statements as if saying them out loud somehow relieved her of guilt. Problem was, I had no idea what she meant, and I was too tired and irritated to sift through her words. "What the hell are you talking about?"

She reached up and swiped at the tears streaming down her cheeks, her words broken and laced with a confusion that rivaled my own. "How are you even here?"

"Storm," I said. "Seems they were moving us out early because the storm knocked out the power to most of the facility. Apparently, that causes a security issue for them."

Carly shook her head as if that information made no sense to her. "He said he confirmed the schedule this morning. You and Cam should still be inside."

"Who is *he*?" Chris ground out, honing in on a detail I hadn't even noticed. "Who, besides you, wanted that other van to stop?"

"The trees were supposed to slow them down, make them come to a stop, not—"

"Wait," I said. "Are you saying you dropped those trees?"

Chris shook his head, grumbling something about me being as stupid as shit and how we should've left her on the side of the road for dead. I ignored him and turned back to Carly, not wanting to believe what she was saying. "You did this?"

She nodded, a fresh round of tears rimming her eyes.

"Who helped you?" I asked. "And why was it so important for you to stop that van?" I couldn't imagine any reason for her to risk her life that way, except to save somebody she knew, somebody she cared about. "Who was on that van?"

"No one I know was on that van," Carly said.

Chris chuckled and tossed the rock he was playing with to the ground. "All right, you want to play semantics—let's play. Who's inside the testing facility that you want to get *to*?"

"Cam," she said. "We did it to get you and Cam out."

ELEVEN

Chris cleared the distance between him and Carly in two strides and grabbed her wrist, forcing her to answer his question. "Who is Cam, and why would you risk all of our lives to get to him?"

"He's her brother." The unfamiliar voice emerged from the woods behind me, and I swung my head in that direction. My eyes landed not on a face, but rather on the rifle he had leveled in our direction. "And I'd strongly suggest," the man continued, his finger slowly inching towards the trigger, "that you take your hands off Carly."

I motioned for Chris to let Carly go, then promptly searched the ground for a rock, a big stick, a giant snowball, something I could use to defend myself. I didn't stand a chance against a rifle, but that didn't mean I was planning on going down easy.

I reached down and grabbed a grisly looking pinecone—the only thing that was within my reach—and started easing my way backward. Chris and I could make a run for it, but the man would easily have time to get off a shot before the woods swallowed us up. That meant only one of us had a chance, and that wasn't a risk I was willing to take. With my life or Chris's.

"Who are you?" I asked, curling my hand around the gnarly pinecone. I searched his face, looking for something familiar about him, a reason to connect him with Carly. The man was old enough to be her father. His clothes were as dirty as Carly's, but they were stained with blood—and from what I could gather, not his own.

I quickly scanned Carly's body again, looking for an injury I might have missed, some indication that this man had caused her harm. But she didn't appear to be scared of him at all. In fact, she seemed relieved to see him.

She jerked her arm free of Chris's hold and walked over to him. Without so much as a second thought, she reached out to lower his gun. The man wavered for a minute, his eyes darting between me and Chris, before he re-engaged the safety and propped his rifle against a nearby tree.

"They won't hurt you," she said, throwing my own words back at me. Funny how that circle-of-trust thing worked. "That's Lucas. Lucas Marshall," she said when the man cocked his head in my direction.

A stunned silence swept over him. "Are there others with them?" he asked as he sidestepped around Carly and searched the area.

"No," Carly said. "How about the vans?"

"I climbed through the wreckage looking for survivors, but the fire … " He paused and swallowed hard before continuing. "The wreckage, the bodies … no one could have walked away from that."

Except us, I almost reminded him.

The man turned around and motioned for whoever was lurking in the woods behind him to step forward. One by one, four guys emerged from the trees. They were my age, their faces poking at memories buried in my mind, ones I couldn't quite grab ahold of. I gave up trying to place their faces and shifted my attention to their hands and the weapons they all seemed to be carrying. Three had axes; one had a two-way radio. No one else had a gun, but somehow that didn't make me feel any better.

As if sensing my confusion, Chris leaned in and whispered, "Do you know these people?"

I shook my head. I didn't know them. I mean, they looked familiar, eerily familiar, but could I place them … yeah, no.

"So run on three?" Chris whispered, and I nodded, trying to figure out a way to communicate my plan to Carly. No way was I leaving here her with a bunch of axe-wielding strangers, no matter how at ease she appeared to be with them.

Chris tapped out the countdown on my leg, and my entire body sprang into action the moment I felt the final beat. I lunged forward and yanked Carly backward, tucking her into my side as I took off running. Chris was beside me, glancing back every few strides to see if they were gaining on us.

Carly twisted in my arms, arguing with me to let her go. I lost my footing and would've stumbled to the ground had something … no, *someone* not reached out to steady me. His sharp intake of breath, followed by a deep rumble of laughter, had me slowly lifting my head, my gaze moving from his tattered jeans to the red plaid shirt sticking out from under his jacket to the black gloved hands still holding me upright.

Chris stopped a few feet ahead of me and spun around, his eyes flaming with fury. I fell backward to the ground with Carly still in my grasp, my thoughts scattering as I did my best to make sense of what I was seeing. *Who* I was seeing. "Nick?"

I watched numbly as he gently placed Carly aside and knelt down in front of me, then stripped off his coat and wrapped it around my shoulders. I couldn't speak, couldn't even mutter a coherent thought.

The five people we'd been running from came barreling though the trees, skidding to a stop when they saw Nick. They fanned out, circling around us, preventing our escape.

"You all right, buddy?" Nick asked as he worked my fingers into his gloves. "You know who I am, right?"

I nodded, both in answer to his question and in disbelief. Nick was my brother's best friend. When Tyler was alive, he'd spent more time at our house than me most days. He still did. Mom liked having him around, said it kept her connected to Tyler.

"I know who you are. You're Nick Meehan. Tyler's best friend," I finally said.

"Well that's a start," he laughed. "You had me worried there for a minute."

With his jacket now off, I could see that he had a gun tucked into the waistband of his jeans. *Two with guns, three with axes, and one with a radio*, I adjusted my mental notes.

Nick sat down next to me and dug through his backpack. He pulled out a first-aid kit and tossed it in Chris's direction, motioning to the gash on his head. "I'd clean that out if I were you. It looks pretty deep."

Chris stayed silent, his hands frozen on the still-unopened first-aid kit.

"He with you?" Nick asked as he opened the kit himself and started tending to the gash on Chris's head.

"Yep," was all I could manage to get out.

"He have a name?" Nick asked.

"Chris," I replied.

"I'm Nick Meehan," he said when I failed to introduce him. "I'm his brother's best friend."

"Fantastic," Chris mumbled under his breath. "And you're here, why?"

"Because I promised his brother I'd look out for him. And that's what I'm doing."

"Umm … you're about a month late," Chris said as he pushed Nick's hands away and smacked a fresh wad of gauze to his head himself. "You should've convinced him to run the day before his seventeenth birthday, before they ever got a chance to test him."

"Probably, and I would've been here sooner, but coordinating with this bunch"—Nick paused, his hand circling to the guys settling to the ground around us—"takes some serious time."

The man who'd leveled his rifle in my direction stepped forward, his hand outstretched. "Joe Thompson. It's nice to finally meet you, Lucas."

I stared at his hand but made no move to take it. I didn't know this guy for shit, and our brief introduction earlier hadn't exactly been friendly.

TWELVE

I dug the heels of my hands into my temples. The headache I'd been nursing since the accident was getting worse, and I didn't know if it was because I was physically hurt or completely and utterly confused. Everybody was staring at me, Chris included, waiting to see what I would do.

"How did you even get here?" I asked. I didn't remember seeing so much as a squirrel on our trip down the mountain, never mind a car.

"We drove," Nick replied, thumbing his finger over his shoulder. "Car's parked about a mile south of here on an old logging trail. We didn't want to risk being seen. No chance of getting either of you out if that happened."

"Ooookay," I said, my eyes darting between the five strangers now spread out around me and Chris. "So you were planning on breaking Cam out?" I shook my head at the impossibility of it all. I'd been there. Lived there. Encased in two rows of electrified fencing and four watchtowers, that place had electronically sealed doors and no windows. And

Taser guns. It wasn't designed simply to keep us in, but to keep the rest of the world out. "With a bunch of strangers?"

"Cam *and* you," Nick corrected. "And they're not strangers." He gestured to the four boys to move closer. "Do you recognize any of them? Do any of them look remotely familiar to you?"

"Nope," I lied. They looked familiar enough, but with the exception of Nick and Carly, I couldn't put a name to a single face.

Nick nodded, and one by one they stood up and rattled off their names.

"Keith. We played on the same little league team in fourth grade. Catcher."

"Second base," the one next to him said. "I'm Connor. We never played on the same team, but your sister Suzie and my sister Julia are in the same kindergarten class."

"In seventh grade some jackass stole all my clothes out of my gym locker when I was in the shower," the third guy said. "You found me sitting in the locker room four hours later, wearing nothing but a towel. You gave me your baseball uniform to wear home, then went and kicked the shit out of the jerk who did it. Name's David, by the way"

Him, I suddenly remembered. "David Reinhart," I said, and he smiled before glancing at the guy next to him.

"Andrew," the next one said without prompting. "I'm the guy you kicked the shit out of."

I shrugged, not an ounce of guilt surfacing. He had it coming.

"Every single one of them knows you, knows Cam," Carly said. "And they jumped at the chance to help."

I stared at them, stunned. There was no common denominator here. No reason for any of them to exhibit that level of loyalty. I barely knew them, and yet here they were, willing to risk their lives to save mine.

"Why now?" I asked, pissed that it was me and not Tyler who had prompted Nick's sudden action. "Why not when my brother was taken?"

"Because Cam's not coming home," Carly replied. "We got the letter two days ago. Because of what they *think* he did, because of what those stupid tests did to him, they're never going to let him come home."

"So you think you can just waltz in there? You do understand how crazy you sound, right? It's not like they issue visitor passes or coordinate family days. That place is essentially a prison, one giant solitary confinement ward."

I spun around to see Chris. He was chuckling to himself, thought their plan was as idiotic as I did. "Do you even remember someone named Cam, because I sure as hell don't."

"Can you name one other person on our hall besides me?" Chris asked.

I looked away, not wanting to risk him seeing the shame in my eyes. There were eight other kids who'd lived on our hall, eight kids who'd listened to me spout off yesterday in our little feel-good therapy session. I'd eaten my meals with them every day, shared a communal bathroom with them, even watched them break down into tears on more than one occasion as they barely survived a test. Yet with the exception of Chris, I didn't know a single one of their names, never took the time to ask.

"My point exactly," Chris said, then turned toward Carly. "Yeah, I know who your brother is. And I doubt he's coming home anytime soon, I can tell you that much."

"Why not?" I asked as I cycled through the faces of every guy I'd ever met in that facility. I didn't remember anyone who looked even remotely like Carly.

"Remember the guy across the hall, the one who snapped and hung his roommate a few days in?" Chris asked.

I nodded. I'd never actually met the guy. Sure, we'd been processed though the same intake center and shared an initial van ride up to the Bake Shop, but he'd kept to himself, never looked up, never made eye contact with any of us. Once inside the testing facility, he became a virtual shut-in, refusing to leave his room until the guards physically hauled him out. The whole building went into lockdown the night he killed his roommate, each of us confined to our room for what seemed like an eternity as the guards screamed orders to each other. The next morning, the door to the room across the hall from ours was wide open, the ten-by-ten-foot space completely empty.

"What about him?" I asked.

"Yeah, that's Cam." Chris replied.

"My brother didn't kill anybody," Carly yelled. "Cameron isn't like that. He gets straight A's in school. He's a camp counselor in the summer and the senior class president. He's not a bad person. They did that to him. They turned him into a monster, and now they're refusing to let him come home."

"They or the gene?" Chris asked.

"They," I replied, not wanting to think about that question. Nature versus nurture. It was a debate I'd been having with myself since the day they took Tyler away. A debate that would haunt me until the day I died.

"Who's to say he's even still there?" I continued. I hadn't heard any mention of the guy since he'd snapped. I assumed they'd transferred him out to a real prison, one where they housed murderers awaiting trial.

"He's in there," Chris said. "There are isolation cells on the lower level of the facility for special people like him."

"And you know that how?"

Chris shrugged. "I pay attention, listen to what the guards are saying to each other, and actually *talk* to the other guys in there with us. You should try it sometime, Lucas. It's amazing the amount of information you can find out when you actually take the time to open your mouth and ask questions."

"Whatever," I said, giving him my middle finger. "I wasn't there to make friends."

"Doesn't matter," Chris said, his words directed to the six people Carly seemed to think could accomplish the impossible. "There's no way you're getting inside that facility. Lucas is right—the place is like Fort Knox."

One of the guys held up his axe, a disturbing grin crossing his face.

"You don't have a chance in hell, not even with that," Chris replied, shaking his head. "Once they see you, they'll start shooting. The guards inside may only be armed with

Taser guns, but the ones in the towers, they're carrying rifles. You can't break into that place. No one can."

"If what you're saying is true and he's still in there, if there's a chance he's still alive, then we have to at least try," Carly said.

Chris grumbled something under his breath, and I instinctively knew what he was thinking—neither one of us was sure that Cam belonged at home, not after what he'd done.

"Do you have any idea what you're asking these guys to do?" Chris turned and sought out the boy next to him. Keith, I think. "Do you have any idea what it's like in there? Did you even stop to consider for a second what will happen when they find out who you are?"

Axe-boy jerked his head as if he knew damn well what he was up against.

"They all risked a lot to come here, Lucas," Carly said, completely ignoring Chris's questions. "They left their families, their friends, their lives behind to help you and Cam." As if that was supposed to sway me in some way.

"Help Cam? *Help* him?" The brother she'd sent in there and the one she was intending to break out were different. Lethally different. "He killed someone, Carly. Even if you did get him out, what do you expect to do with him?"

Nick sighed, his eyes meeting mine. "You honestly believe Cam is capable of hurting someone? Carly's brother. Olivia's brother. You honestly believe he could kill someone?"

"If you asked me three years ago if my brother would ever commit suicide, I'd tell you that you were insane. But that place changes you, turns you into someone you'd barely even recognize. So, yeah. I think there's a good chance he did it."

THIRTEEN

"We weren't planning on forcing our way in, Lucas. At least not exactly." Joe Thompson, who'd been letting Nick take the lead, now stepped forward and pointed methodically at each guy. "How old do they look to you?"

I did a quick scan of their faces. I knew Nick's age, Carly's too. The rest of them ... didn't know, didn't care. "My age, I guess. Why?"

"What day of the week did you get transported to the testing facility?" Joe asked.

"Tuesday," Chris and I answered in unison. 4:03 p.m., to be exact. I remembered the moment we'd pulled into the Bake Shop. We were herded into a padded waiting room, where they verified our names and dates of birth. One by one they led us up into a small examining room and strip-searched us, three guards looking on as they checked in places no sane human being would think to hide stuff. It was humiliating, intentionally so, and I nearly took a swing at the guard myself when he asked me to drop my pants.

"And how about Tyler?" Nick asked, pulling me from that memory. "Do you remember what day it was when they showed up for him?"

Unfortunately, I did. I could still hear the sound of their tires on our stone driveway growing louder as they approached, small rocks sputtering onto the lawn. They'd knocked on the door, and when I didn't answer it fast enough, they broke it down, trained their weapons at Tyler's chest, and cuffed him. All because Tyler was in the bathroom and Mom was on the phone begging Sheriff Watts to intervene. He didn't. No one intervened on Tyler's behalf. Or mine.

"Tuesday," I finally replied. "9:02 in the morning."

"And Cam?" Joe asked Carly.

She didn't need to answer; I already knew what he was getting at. There was only one road leading to the Bake Shop, and Tuesday was the transportation day.

"I knew that IGT transfer van was carrying four boys and one guard, plus their driver," Joe said. "I know everything about the facility, right down to how thick the walls are and who won the bid to construct it. I sat on the Government Task Force for Violent Crimes for ten years and was privy to every discussion they had about how to effectively manage MAOA-L carriers. I was one of the few who voiced opposition to the construction of these facilities, and I was dismissed from the Task Force because of my views. But that didn't stop me from watching what was going on and tracking every move IGT made. For the last two years, I've studied every bit of information I could get my hands on, hacked into their systems, and collected volumes of information about the kids they're testing.

I've done my homework, Lucas. And I'm done with waiting for Washington to figure out what I already know. These facilities and IGT's testing protocols are only succeeding in destroying the lives of boys just like you. Just like Tyler. Just like Cam."

"And you, what, heard about Cam and figured Carly would be the perfect person to help you?" I asked, pissed that Joe was using Carly's fear and grief against her. "Carly is all the Dentons have left. Olivia's gone. Cam is pretty much gone, but you've dragged her up here anyway."

"Cam's not gone," Carly whispered back, her eyes welling with tears. "And that's exactly why I went to Mr. Thompson. Dad tried to reason with the testing facility's administrators. He talked to our congressman, even tried to get the press involved, but nobody would listen. Nobody cared. So when I saw Mr. Thompson on TV, protesting the construction of more facilities, I tracked him down, begged him to help. I didn't know what else to do."

I understood her desperation. I'd lived through it myself two years ago when Tyler tested positive and my mother's world—my world—fell out from under me. But even knowing how screwed-up that place was, I would never want my own sister, never mind a bunch of innocent guys from my school, risking their lives to save mine.

"And you?" I asked, turning toward Nick. "How are you involved in all this?"

"I told you. I promised Tyler I'd look out for you. So when Carly and Joe came to me, I signed on, no questions asked."

"So you were simply planning on swapping these four guys for the four on the van?" I'd figured out their plan and was amazed at the idiocy of the whole idea. "You thought it'd be super easy and you could just literally drive through the front gate?"

Joe nodded, and I continued. "What about the guard and the driver?"

"Why do you think I brought Nick?" Joe replied, as if it all made perfect sense. "Four boys, one guard, one driver."

A rumble of laughter erupted from Chris's chest as he stood up and dramatically spun around, his arms wide, the smile covering his face more mocking than amused. "You guys are stupider than I thought. Do you notice anything similar about me and Lucas? Anything at all?"

They stared at Chris, not catching what he was inferring. I stood up and went to stand next to him, hoping my proximity would clue them in. First thing the guards did before they transferred you from the intake center to the testing facility was take your clothes and replace them with IGT-issued jeans, white T-shirts, and gray hoodies. Hell, even the boxers I was sporting had the IGT logo stamped on the inside. The four guys Joe had recruited for this stupid mission were wearing a wide array of bright colors, jackets, and thermal gloves. None of which would get them past the front gate.

It took Joe a few seconds, but his eyes eventually lit with recognition, a muffled curse falling from his lips. Despite everything he knew about the Bake Shop, he somehow hadn't planned on facility-issued clothing, hadn't even realized Chris and I were dressed exactly the same until we'd pointed it out.

"They're dead, you know. Every single one of them. Dead. Because of you," I said.

"I never meant for anyone to get hurt. I promise you, that was the last thing I wanted." Joe shifted his feet against the frozen ground, his eyes never lifting to meet mine. "I came to get you out, to get all of them out. I found a back door into IGT's transportation logs. I checked it last night, and again this morning before I dragged them up here. There was no mention of an outbound van heading to the reintegration facility. If there was, I wouldn't have risked it. What happened back on that road was an accident. A horrible, tragic accident, Lucas, but nothing more."

The guy looked genuinely upset, but that didn't mean I believed him, didn't mean I was about to place my trust—or my life—in his hands.

"And the boys on the van … where were you planning on stashing them after you stole their van and impersonated their lives?"

Nick yanked the zipper of his backpack open and turned it upside down. A blanket, a compressed sleeping bag, and at least a dozen protein bars spilled out onto the snow.

"We weren't planning on being in there more than a few hours, Lucas. Definitely not long enough for them to freeze to death or anything," Nick said as he pulled a pack of zip-ties out of his back pocket. "We were just going to detain them for a little while and borrow their van."

"Well, that plan went to shit, now didn't it?" Chris mocked as he snagged a fistful of granola bars from the stash. He tossed one my way, then opened one for himself before shoving the rest into the pocket of his sweatshirt.

"So what's your plan now?" Chris continued, through a mouthful of granola. "How exactly are you proposing to get inside without a facility-issued van or clothing?"

And once you're in, how the hell do you plan on getting back out, I silently added.

"And what about Carly?" I asked. "Are you planning on just leaving her here in the woods to fend for herself until you get back?"

"Nope," Carly answered. "I'm going in there with them."

"There wasn't a single girl on that van," Chris said. He had no idea who was on the transfer van, really, but given the fact that only one girl in the entire history of the program had ever tested positive for MAOA-L, it was a safe assumption. "How were you going to explain your sudden appearance?" he went on. "Girls don't test positive for the gene—"

"That's not true," Carly interrupted. "One has."

She'd done her homework, I'd give her that. But the government had questioned the results of the girl who'd tested positive, stunned that a female was carrying what they'd assumed was a male-only gene mutation.

"And you expect them to believe you're the second one?" I asked.

"Maybe," Carly replied

"That's bullshit, and you know it," Chris fired back. "One quarter of the population carries the warrior gene, and of that, only a tiny of fraction test positive for the MAOA-L mutation. A girl … well, you'd have a better chance of getting struck by lightning while fighting off a shark attack than you do of testing positive. Trust me, if a second girl had tested positive, the entire world would know about it. There's no way that information wouldn't have made national news by now. She'd pretty much be every scientist's wet dream."

It was a crude analogy, but Chris was right. "You showing up at all is gonna tip the guards off to that fact that something is wrong," I said.

"They won't know. Not right away, anyway," Nick countered. "We have papers for her, ones we forged. Sure, in a couple of days they'll figure it out, but we aren't planning on being there for more than a few hours tops."

Carly looked to me for help. I shrugged my shoulders. There wasn't much I could do. Chris was right. Her chances of getting in there were slim to none.

"Then there's got to be another way," Carly said. "We can't just leave Cam in there. I won't. I can't."

I understood her desire to rescue her brother, but I wouldn't risk what little I had left of my own life to save his. "It's not possible, Carly. Trust me. I've spent a month living inside that place; it's not happening."

"I wouldn't say that," Nick said, and I glanced in his direction, oddly curious to see what half-baked plan he was cooking up now. "The power is down across this whole area," he mused out loud. "A transformer went down about ten miles south of here. I gotta think it will take at least a few days to get it up and running. That could buy us some time."

"Buy you time to do what?" I asked, not seeing where he was going with any of this. "You planning on jogging to the local Wal-Mart and outfitting yourselves to look like us?"

Nick laughed, sounding more annoyed than amused.

"Think, Lucas. If the power is out, then my guess is most of their security systems are down as well. We could walk right in there and take him. Who the hell cares about forged documents or switching these four guys out for the ones on that van. We don't need their help anymore."

"Let's forget about how stupid that plan is for a second," Chris chimed in. "Are you forgetting about the backup generators? The ones that keep the lights on and their security system intact?"

"No, Nick is right," Carly said, completely dismissing Chris's concerns. "You told me they moved you out early because of the storm, that they were worried about security with the power down, yes?"

"Yeah, so?"

"Well, if there's no power—"

"They're running basic utilities, counting solely on the guards to keep order," Joe said, finishing her thought. "The question is, can we kill the generators and slip in unnoticed?"

"Technically, the generators could be down as long as you need them to be," Chris replied. "It's easy enough to disable them if you know what you're doing."

"And do you?" Nick asked, his smile hinting at the plan he was obviously constructing on the spot.

A disturbing grin crept across Chris's face. I didn't know much about Chris's past, but I'd learned he had some mad skills when it came to electronics and was the nightmare of his school's tech department. My guess was, something as simple as knocking out a generator wouldn't be a problem for him.

"I could keep them down for the next week if I wanted to,

but I have no intention of helping you," Chris told Nick, and I sighed in relief. For a minute there, I'd thought he was signing onto this insanity.

"I'm with Chris," I said as I walked over to the pile of supplies Nick had emptied from his backpack and grabbed the sleeping bag. I was cold and tired of listening to them go on about their asinine plan. "No way am I getting involved in this. No way in hell."

Carly's hand banded around my arm. "What's wrong with you?" she yelled, her fingers tightening to a near painful level. "How can you not even consider helping us? They basically killed your brother. My sister. And now they have Cam."

"Even if we could get him out, Carly, he wouldn't be the same. Do you get that? Do you have any idea how messed up your brother truly is? Because I do." I'd seen it with Tyler, and he hadn't even killed anybody.

"I don't care," she said. "He's still my brother. He deserves a chance."

I tossed that warped concept around in my mind for a half second before waving her off. "You have no idea how hard it is to survive that place. No clue! And what you're asking me to do . . . " I paused and fanned my hand out in Chris's direction. "What you're asking us to do will take away any chance we have of a normal life. And for what? To save your brother?"

"You weren't born evil, Lucas. Neither was Tyler or Cam," Joe said.

He wasn't telling me anything I didn't already know. No matter how many times they'd labeled me potentially violent or how many tests they'd put me through, I'd never once bought into their gene theory. If you asked me, the whole idea of trying to figure out who had psychotic potential was about as reliable as playing darts blindfolded. Regardless of the odds, if you kept on throwing, eventually you'd hit the target. Problem was, the target they'd set their sights on this time was me.

"In the country I grew up in," Joe added, "we didn't put people away solely on the idea that maybe, *someday*, they might do something wrong."

I took a deep breath. "Then perhaps you should move," I said. "Because that's exactly what this country is doing."

FOURTEEN

"Let's look at it this way, Lucas," Joe said. "I'm not asking you to risk your lives to sneak Cam out; I'm just asking you to help *me* get inside. I can show them the results I've compiled from my research, convince them to rethink what they're doing. Maybe they'll give Cam, and everyone like him, a second chance."

"They took your brother, the one person my sister ever loved," Carly added, sliding to the ground next to me and burying her feet beneath my sleeping bag. "And because of what they did to Tyler, I lost my sister. They may not have physically put the razor blade in her hand, but it's their fault all the same. And now they have Cam. How long do you think it'll be before they take someone else we know? Someone else we love?"

It was that "someone else" comment that had me burying my head in my hands and considering, for half a second, helping them.

"It's a waste of time," Chris insisted. "There are only a

handful of guards in there, but they aren't going to be interested in helping you. They hate us as much as the rest of the world does. And that counselor couldn't care less about Joe's research or what happens to us."

"You mean Anne? Anne Tremblay?" Joe asked. "I know her. She's the reason I chose to infiltrate your facility instead of one of the others; it's one of the main reasons I agreed to help Carly. Anne will listen to me. I assure you, she will. With my research files and her testimony, we can make a case to Washington and have all the facilities shut down permanently. But I need to get inside. I just need five minutes of her time to show her what I've learned.

I laughed; I couldn't help it. If that idiot was banking on Ms. Tremblay helping us, then he was dumber than I thought. "And what makes you think she gives a damn about any of us?" I asked, remembering the countless times she'd stood watch as they poked and prodded at our willpower, her eyes always focused on that stupid tablet she carried around to record our results. "We're nothing but data to her."

"Not true, Lucas. Her husband was a criminal psychologist. She is too. We worked together on the Government Task Force for Violent Crimes. At first, she was as vehemently opposed to these facilities as I was. She vowed to never see a single one of them constructed."

"Umm hmm," I mumbled, not for a second buying that lie. "If that's true, then tell me—what changed her mind? Because I can guarantee she hates us as much as the rest of the world."

"The death of her husband," Joe said. "And of her daughter."

In all the times Ms. Tremblay had tried to get us to open up about ourselves, about our families, she'd never once mentioned a husband or daughter of her own.

"If you know Ms. Tremblay so well, if she's so trustworthy, then why do this? Why not just pick up the damn phone and call her?" Chris asked.

"You think I haven't tried that? You think I'd drag these kids out here and endanger their lives if there was any other way?"

I shrugged. If I was being honest, then yes, that was exactly what I thought.

"I haven't seen or talked to her in nearly three years, Lucas. Not since the funeral. Not since I learned she'd signed onto the project. The calls I've tried to place to her have been ignored or sent to a dead voicemail."

"Then wait until her six-week stint in there is done, have her over for a dinner, and lay out your evidence," Chris offered up. "I don't know about you, but that kinda feels like a more logical plan to me."

"Sure, that would be nice if it were remotely possible. But the information going into the facility is as tightly controlled as the information coming out. Anne has pretty much been forbidden to talk to me, or to any other member of the Task Force that voiced dissent over the testing protocols."

"So, what … if she won't willingly talk to you, then you figure the best—the *only*—alternative is to lie your way in, force her to listen to you?"

"That's exactly what I plan to do. It's the only way."

"Well, good luck to you," Chris said as he settled into a sleeping bag next to me. "Can't wait to hear how that plan turns out for you."

FIFTEEN

It was dark, the shadow of the moon behind the clouds casting an eerie glow across the snow. Chris was lying next to me, his breathing labored as he struggled to stay warm. The blankets and sleeping bags Nick had brought with him did little to stave off the chill, never mind insulate us from the cold, wet ground.

My body needed rest, but my mind refused to let go. Every time I closed my eyes, Tyler's face would merge with Cam's, twisting together as a tormented scream ripped from their communal throat, sending me bolting upright.

The nightmares about Tyler I could handle; they'd been my nightly companions for the last two years. It was this new dream about Chris and Suzie that had me fighting for air.

Chris blindfolded, his arms and legs strapped to a chair as they sent pulses of high-pitched frequency through the earbuds crammed into his ears. His face screwed up in agony as he clawed at the zip-ties, begging to be set free. His head fell forward in defeat as I walked toward him, intent on releasing his binds. But when I undid the blindfold and he raised his eyes to meet mine, it wasn't Chris staring back at me, but rather Suzie, silently pleading with me for help.

"Fine," I yelled out, physically shaking off that last dream. "I'll do it."

"Be sure about this," Chris grumbled next to me. I hadn't known he was awake, but I couldn't say I was surprised. He was as prone to night terrors as me lately.

"I'm sure," I said, understanding his words for what they were. If I was signing onto Joe's plan to infiltrate the facility, then he was coming with me.

I sat up, searching the darkened area for Joe. I found him a few feet away, leaning against a tree, his rifle propped on his shoulder, keeping watch. "I'll do it. I'll help you get your information to Ms. Tremblay. But it won't work the way you were planning. Both vans are gone, including the guards' uniforms and the IGT-issued clothing."

"I'm listening." Joe straightened up and inched closer. "What are you thinking?"

"There's no way you can slip into that place unnoticed. Forget the two row of fences and the armed guards in the towers; every corridor in there is monitored, and there's a camera in every room. Power may be down, but the staff is still there, still armed, still watching. So you can't get in. But the two of us can."

"And we need Carly," Chris said. "She's our ticket inside."

It was true. The guards at that facility were mean, I'd give you that, but I doubted they were cruel enough leave a poor, innocent girl stranded outside the front gate with us as her sole company.

"We can play her off as some random girl we picked up along the way. Tell them we hit her car and miraculously, the three of us walked away," Chris suggested.

"Exactly," I said. Chris's plan was perfect and completely in line with mine. We didn't need to sneak ourselves in; we belonged in there. And Carly ... well, she was the pity card we'd play with Ms. Tremblay.

"No way," Joe argued. "There's no way I'm letting you take Carly in there unarmed and without me to keep her safe. Without me to keep you all safe."

If he gave a shit about her safety, then he wouldn't have dragged her up here at all, I thought to myself.

"I'm with Joe on this one," Nick added. "I'm all for leaving the other guys behind, but there's no way I'm letting you walk back into that place without me at your back. You know better than anyone what that place is capable of. I was there the day you buried Tyler, the day the Dentons buried Olivia. You honestly think I'll let you drag Carly in there without me?"

"You're only two years older than me, Nick. Two. And I hate to tell you this, but Chris and I are the only ones who know how that place works. I'll go along with this stupid idea of Joe's—I'll even try and get Cam out and hand-deliver the research to Ms. Tremblay—but I'm taking Carly in there with us. Only her."

I hadn't exactly come to this conclusion without considering everything that could go wrong. The Bake Shop was full of teenage boys, all being subjected to tests deliberately designed to break their control. And the half-dozen, trigger-happy guards who lived there worked on six-week cycles, so the only woman they'd seen this month was the rather unimpressive Ms. Tremblay; adding Carly to that mix of amped-up testosterone was a risk I wasn't looking forward to taking. But if this was going to work, then yes, that's exactly what I expected Nick and Joe to let me do.

"Only her," I said, restating my position.

"She's the only daughter the Dentons have left, Lucas," Nick argued.

"We won't let anything happen to her," I said, fully aware of how hollow that promise was. Chris and I would be lucky to get ourselves out alive, never mind protect Carly.

I searched out the darkness surrounding me for Carly, knowing for a fact I could sway her to my side. She'd do just about anything to get to her brother, including leaving Joe and his collection of weapons behind. "You want my help getting your brother out, then this is the only way you're going to get it. You in?"

"Absolutely," she responded.

"It's just going to be you, me, and Chris. Nobody else. We're not bringing any weapons with us, not so much as a rock. I can't guarantee we'll be able to get Cam out, but—"

"I know," Carly interrupted. "But he's all I have left. After what happened to Olivia, I can't lose him too. I need to at least try."

"Good. Because if what you're saying about Cam is true— if they broke him the way they broke Tyler—then I'm not sure he'll listen to anybody but you."

SIXTEEN

The sun was barely making its appearance the following morning as we set out for the Bake Shop, each of us lost in our own thoughts. There was no point in sleeping. No amount of rest, no amount of plotting, could prepare us for what we were about to do. And lying on the cold, wet ground, with nothing but my own thoughts to keep me company, was the last thing I needed.

There was a good chance I'd just signed Carly's death certificate in exchange for the chance to save a guy I didn't even know. A guy I wasn't even sure deserved a second chance. And my sister's future—along with the fate of every person who tested positive from this day forward—rested on the flash drive full of proof I'd tucked in my sock and the moral decency of a counselor I'd come to hate.

I twisted my ankle, trying to dislodge the flash drive from between my toes. Joe had handed it to me earlier that morning, instructing me to give it to nobody but Ms. Tremblay. Inside my sock had seemed like the safest place to keep it, but now, more than three miles into the hike, it was quickly becoming one of the most irritatingly painful decisions I'd ever made.

"You have any idea what's on that thing?" Chris asked when I stopped and sat down in the middle of the road, yanking my shoe off. The flash drive was digging into my big toe, and squirming wasn't doing any good.

"Files. Two years' worth of evidence. Names of families that have been torn apart by the testing program. My life history. Yours."

I wasn't a hundred percent sure what was on the drive; I hadn't exactly had the opportunity to check it out for myself. Joe had rattled of the contents, telling me which files to direct Ms. Tremblay's attention to, which ones he deemed most incriminating. I trusted he was telling the truth—not because I wanted to, but because second-guessing him would make me more paranoid than I already was.

I tucked the drive back into the heel of my sock and stood up, testing to make sure it wouldn't crack under my weight before I laced my sneaker. "Seems like a colossal waste of time if you ask me," I continued. "No clue how he expects Ms. Tremblay to download the information without any power."

"Agreed," Chris replied. "You've seen the way she watches us, like she can't decide whether to fear or pity us."

My guess was both, but I didn't bother to say that. No point in confirming the obvious.

I got up and started walking again despite my body's protest. We'd stopped twice already, and each time I'd felt my temperature dropping. My blood was slowly freezing in my veins. We needed to keep moving.

Carly was a few steps behind us—close enough that she could hear what we were saying but too far away to be part of the conversation. It was intentional, or so I thought. Like she still hadn't fully committed to trusting us. I'd turn around and check on her every few minutes to make sure she wasn't falling behind, but she was always there, always keeping pace with me.

"You know the only reason I agreed to this whole save-Cam-and-trust-Ms.-Tremblay plan is because of you, right?" Chris asked.

"I know," I replied. "And thanks."

"I'd do anything for you," Chris continued, his eyes flashing toward the woods. The driving wind that had kept us huddled in our sleeping bags during the night had completely died down, the snow no longer swirling around. We had a clear view of everything around us, the unmarked snow and pristine sky a stark contrast to the chaos I feared lay ahead of us.

"Anything," Chris repeated, the conviction in his voice momentarily stilling my fear. "But that Nick friend of yours is starting to piss me off, so much so that I may have to tackle him to the ground and pummel some sense into him. He's gonna screw this whole plan to shit if he doesn't get lost."

I caught a glimpse of Nick in the trees and knew the rest of the guys were only steps behind him. Nick had insisted they follow us to the facility, something about wanting to be close by in case anything went wrong. I laughed but didn't argue; if sitting out in the freezing cold would give him a sense of control, then so be it.

They'd promised they'd stay out of sight the entire way, on the off-chance that the facility had sent out a search party for the vans. I'd given Nick back his jacket before we set off, afraid that showing up wearing anything other than the clothes we'd left in would make the guards suspicious. Damn jacket was bright red and did little to keep him hidden; it glinted off the snow like a homing beacon, drawing my attention away from the snowdrifts we were snaking our way around and straight to him.

"And what's up with her?" Chris continued, motioning to Carly. "You'd think she could at least walk with us, given what we're risking to save her brother. A 'thank you' would be nice too."

I shrugged. "She's nervous, that's all." Carly wasn't nervous; she was scared as hell. She'd read Tyler's journal, knew exactly what she was walking into. And it wasn't good.

"Nah, it's more than that." Chris put his hand on my arm, drawing me to a stop. "She doesn't like me. Here I am, risking my ass to save her brother, and she can't even look me in the eye and say thank you. If you ask me, that's the reason Nick is following us. Carly doesn't trust me, and neither does he. You'd think she would at least have questions about to what to expect."

Chris wasn't exactly wrong, but telling him that, and adding more tension to an already explosive situation, wasn't gonna help. Carly had pulled me aside that morning when Chris was off in the woods peeing and taking care of whatever else he needed to do. She wanted to leave Chris behind, tweak the story so it was her and Nick in the car that hit ours, with me as the only survivor in the van. I was surprised to hear Joe back her up, even offer to watch over Chris himself until we came back out.

I got Carly's fear. She was walking straight into the devil's lair; I'd worry more if she weren't afraid. But what I couldn't understand was her inability to trust me.

"Sometimes it's better to go in blind," I said, hoping Chris would drop the issue and move on. "You know, hold on to the illusion that there's hope for as long as possible. Maybe that's what she's doing."

"That's the worst advice I've ever heard," Chris said as he clapped me on the back. The sound, combined with my grunt of annoyance, drew Nick's attention. He stepped out onto the road and motioned for us to shut up.

"Give me a minute," I said as I waved Chris forward and waited for Carly to catch up.

"What?" she asked as I fell into step behind her.

"Of all the people volunteering to go back in with me, I chose Chris to have my back. Not Nick, not Joe. Only Chris. There's a reason for that." I didn't bother to explain what was behind the strength of our bond. "I trust him with my life, and if you're smart, you will too."

"He's convinced that my brother—the same brother who taught me how to bait a fishing hook and drive a car—is so messed up that he isn't even worth saving. And you want me to trust him? Believe that he'll actually try and save Cam?"

She'd pretty much summed it up, and to be honest, my line of thinking wasn't all that different from Chris's when it came to Cam. "Yep, that's exactly what I expect."

We walked in silence for the next half hour, noting the

occasional hawk that kept us company. Every tree, every snowdrift, every rock looked the same. For all I knew, we'd been walking in circles, never getting more than a few hundred yards from where we'd spent the night. Waste of energy. Waste of time.

The road narrowed to one lane, the snowdrifts so high that I wondered if the road was even passable. I squinted against the blinding sunlight to the gate up ahead. There was a *No Trespassing* sign affixed to the front. It was swinging, the noise of the thin metal colliding with the rail echoing through the dead space around us.

I remembered those metal bars, distinctly recalled the guard in our van having to get out and manually pull the gate open when we left because the power was down. The fence here wasn't electrified, but it wouldn't matter if it were. This three-foot-high gate was meant as a warning, not a deterrent. The real barricade was a quarter-mile ahead: twelve feet tall and juiced up with enough electricity to kill you instantly.

"Are we here?" Carly asked.

I nodded. "It's up over that rise. You're positive you want to do this?" If she had any hesitation, she needed to back out right then, because once we stepped foot on the facility's grounds, I needed her complete and absolute trust. "You're good leaving Nick behind and going in with just me and Chris?"

She wavered, her eyes darting toward the woods where Nick, Joe, and the guys would stay safely hidden in the trees, waiting for us to return.

"Carly?" Her hesitation bothered me, and I half considered calling the whole thing off.

SEVENTEEN

The Bake Shop was enormous—tall and imposing. My eyes wandered, noticing for the first time that there were no trees, no nature of any kind in the enclosed space. It was a steel and cinderblock building constructed on twenty-five acres of concrete, like everything alive had been stripped away in favor of forged metal and stone. Funny how I hadn't focused on that when they'd first brought me here.

With the exception of our footprints, the snow leading up to the fence was unmarred. In my mind, that meant only one thing—they hadn't even bothered to send anybody out looking for us.

"You think it's odd that no cars have come and gone from this place?" I asked Chris.

"Nope. With the main power down, they probably can't spare the manpower. I mean, there's no way they can keep all their security measures up and running on generators alone. My guess is they cut power to the electronic looks in our bunk room and the fence. With no electronic locks to keep us safely tucked in our rooms, there's a higher risk of people going nuts in there. They need all the guards inside, watching over the crazy kids, not out here looking for us."

Made sense, but it bothered me all the same.

I held out my hand to Chris, curling my fingers for the rock we'd been tossing between us our entire hike here. It had kept us amused and prevented our hands from completely freezing, but now it had an even more important purpose, one that would keep us from potentially getting fried.

He handed me the rock and I tossed it at the fence, watching it bounce off the metal links and land on the opposite side, just out of our reach. I didn't see any sparks or hear the zap of power, which was what I was hoping for. Carly, who was hovering near us, looked surprised.

"What the hell did you do that for?" Chris asked, shoving his arm through the fence in an unsuccessful attempt to retrieve his only toy.

"Electric fence," I said.

"No power," he replied. "No way those things are lit up. Any idiot would've known that."

He wiggled his arm, trying to squeeze more of it through the fence, not even coming close to reaching the rock. "Well, that's just fantastic, Lucas. I was planning on chucking that at the door to get their attention."

The only door I could see from our position was sealed shut. No window. No knob. No way in.

"How are we supposed to get in now?" Chris asked.

Having been most concerned with what was going to happen once we were inside, I hadn't considered the fact that there'd be no one out here to announce our arrival to. I'd assumed there'd still be guards posted in the towers, and we'd simply walk up to the front gate and wave at one of them. I didn't think of the possibility that the guards in the towers would've been moved inside, or the fact that there were no windows to even flag somebody down through.

"We need to get their attention," I said as I walked over to the two surveillance cameras mounted on the fence. They were pointed down, the flashing red lights off.

"They probably turned off the outside cameras to save generator power," Chris said, confirming what I'd already figured out.

"Yep. So how do we get in?" I walked the perimeter of the fence, searching for a window, a hole in the fence's links, a random security guard out on patrol, but found nothing. Not a squirrel, not even a downed limb. I considered yelling, but I knew for a fact those walls were completely soundproof. I mean, if Cam could strangle his screaming roommate across the hall from us without either me or Chris hearing, then I'd say those walls were pretty damn solid.

Chris settled on the ground by the main gate, Carly taking a seat a few feet away from him. I walked over and slid down next to them. With the Bake Shop locked up tight, we had no other option but to wait.

I slipped my sneaker off and rubbed at my frozen foot until it started aching again. It wasn't black—yet—and at least I could still feel it. "Son of a bitch," I ground out as the circulation rushed back into my toes, the pain intensifying to an excruciating level. "It's cold out here."

"It's been cold for the last twenty-four hours," Chris fired back. "Where the hell have you been?"

I ignored him and went about removing my other sneaker. My socks were soaking wet, the navy blue dye streaking my feet and giving them a morbid appearance.

"You do get how absolutely hysterical this is, don't you?" Chris asked as he watched me cradling my foot. "They take us from our family and friends, on some stupid assumption that we could be dangerous, and lock us up. They secure this place to the hilt to make sure we can't get out, submit us to a battery of tests, and—"

"And yet here we are, two potential psychopaths, sitting on the ground, tired and half frozen, on the *outside*," I said, finishing his thought. It was insanely ironic and completely absurd.

"I don't get what's so funny," Carly said.

"They've locked us out," Chris replied. "The government spent millions of taxpayer dollars trying to keep the general population safe from our kind, and here we are, trapped outside their walls with all you innocent victims at our disposal."

"Kind of makes you want to do something stupid just to make a point, doesn't it?" I replied.

"No, it doesn't, and sitting here laughing about it isn't helping anything," Carly snapped. "We need to find a way to get in."

I wanted to get in just as badly as she did. Now that I was sitting here, a few yards away from a warm bed and hot food, the cold I'd refused to acknowledge bore into my bones. I didn't care what awaited us inside, what they'd do to me, or how many lies I would have to tell—I just wanted in.

"What did you have in mind then, sweetheart?" Chris's drawl was intentional and sickeningly sweet. He was as tired and irritated as me and not above amusing himself at Carly's expense.

"I don't know." Carly scanned the exterior of the building, looking for an access point she'd never find. "Maybe there's a window in the back or another rock we could throw at the door. You said the main power was down and they wouldn't want to waste generator power electrifying the fence, so maybe we just climb over."

I pointed to the top of the fence I was leaning against. "See that mass of wire up there? That's razor wire. It'll tear you to shreds, but feel free to give it a try and let me know how it goes."

She huffed out a response I couldn't quite understand and went back to her pointless surveying of the facility's impenetrable walls.

"You want me to do something?" Chris mocked. "All right, I'll do something. How about this?"

He stood up and walked a few feet away to a clean patch of snow. I barely controlled my laughter as he unzipped his fly and pissed out *WE'RE BACK*. "That should catch their attention, don't you think?"

I didn't bother to point out that the cameras were off and there wasn't a window in the entire building. If it made Chris feel better to pee out his aggression, then that was fine by me.

EIGHTEEN

I would've kept on laughing, completely oblivious to the Bake Shop's door opening, if Carly hadn't jabbed me in the ribs. I jumped to my feet and spun around, scouring my brain for the story all three of us had memorized. I came up empty, fear stealing my words.

I wrapped my hands around the links of the fence and leaned in. I couldn't make out the face of the person standing by the door. Whoever it was had their back to us, as if trying to shelter their face from the driving cold.

"Ms. Tremblay," Chris whispered, and I nodded as my eyes trailed down to the heels she always wore—dull and gray, just like the facility.

She took a few steps away from the safety of the building and lifted her cellphone into the air. We were smack in the center of a no man's land and she honestly thought she could get a signal. Idiot.

"So once we get in, we should—"

Carly took off running along the fence before I even

finished my sentence. So much for the warning I'd given her about trusting Chris and me.

"She's gonna get us killed," Chris hissed, darting after her. His fingers grazed the hood of her jacket. He yanked hard, and she fell backward into the snow.

It was that sound—the thump of Carly landing on her butt, followed by the string of curses she launched in Chris's direction—that caught Ms. Tremblay's attention.

"What in the—" Ms. Tremblay slapped a hand over her mouth. Her eyes widened as she realized that she wasn't alone, that Chris and I were standing on the other side of the fence, completely unsecured in the outside world.

I smiled, a bit of smug satisfaction settling in. Ms. Tremblay hadn't planned on ever having to see me again. And definitely not without all of the fancy electronic locks and Taser-armed guards to keep her safe.

I waved, my smile anything but friendly.

"Lucas? Chris? What are you doing here?" The question was directed at us, but her eyes never left Carly. Her gaze ran the entire length of Carly's body, searching for some indication that she was hurt. There were a couple of scratches on Carly's hands and a day's worth of dirt ground into her clothes, but other that, I'd say she looked pretty damn good.

Ms. Tremblay took a step toward us, her tone softening, her eyes sympathetic as she curled her fingers around the fence. Something about the look on her face bothered me. Maybe it was the way her focus lingered on Carly's scrapes rather than Chris's bloody head.

"Are you okay?" she finally asked Carly, her shoulders

stiffening as she sent an accusing glare in my direction. "Did they hurt you?"

That last question pissed me off beyond belief. For weeks I'd listened to her spout off her psycho-babble bullshit, promising us that she was here to help us adjust, become more comfortable expressing ourselves with words instead of violence. And her first glimpse of me and Chris on the outside had her condemning us as predators. It didn't matter how many tests we'd passed for them; in their minds—in *her* mind—we'd always be dangerous.

Little did she know that Chris and I were the only innocent ones here. Little Miss Perfect was responsible for the deaths of over a dozen people.

"We didn't touch her," Chris barked, obviously as angry as me.

Ms. Tremblay ignored him, her attention still solely focused on Carly. "I'm going to go inside and get one of the guards. Don't worry, I'll be right back. You'll be safe here."

"You got to be kidding me," I mumbled under my breath. Carly was bundled up in a winter jacket and boots, with nothing wrong but some pine needles twisted into her hair and a dirty coat. But Chris and I were a wreck. His head was caked with dried blood, my shoulder was killing me, and neither one of us had more than a thin sweatshirt on. Still, Ms. Tremblay's first concern was for Carly.

"Wait! There was a crash," Carly called after her, launching into our well-rehearsed lie. "Their van collided with my car and then rolled over the cliff. My car did too."

"Shut up!" Chris yelled at Carly. Our plan was to get

inside, then stall for as long as we could before telling them the whole story. We were hoping to buy ourselves some time to look around and figure out how bad things had gotten before explaining our sudden reappearance. Apparently, though, Carly missed the memo. Or she was making up her own plan as she went along.

I walked over to Carly and whispered, "Save some of that information until after we get inside."

Carly shook her head and inched closer to the fence. "I was trying to find my dad's hunting cabin, but I must have taken a wrong turn. I got lost and then … then … " She trailed off, her eyes skirting over me and Chris. "I don't know where I am. I don't know who they are. I just need to use a phone. I need to call my dad and let him know where I am."

"Enough!" Chris reached out for her, but I held him back, curious to see how far Carly would take this. That, and her plan was actually working; Ms. Tremblay had finally shifted her attention to me and Chris, her face paling as she took in our injuries.

"How did you get here?" she asked.

"We walked," I answered.

Ms. Tremblay looked past me to the road, quickly realizing what I already knew. There were no tire tracks, no flashing blue and red lights; just three solitary sets of footprints in the otherwise undisturbed snow. "Nobody stopped to help you? You made it all the way back here on your own?"

I nodded. "It's not like there was a 7-Eleven we could've walked into and asked for help. You picked a good place to build this facility. Out in the woods, away from people, away from any kind of help should an accident occur and leave a bunch kids like me and Chris hurt and alone."

Ms. Tremblay gave a small, sympathetic nod. So far, so good.

"We followed the road back here. We didn't know what else to do," I finished, hunching over and groaning in pain for effect.

"There was a van that was supposed to be heading up here. It had four boys on it, along with two guards. We assume they waited at the intake facility until the storm passed—the phones are down so we can't verify that. Did you pass them on the road? Did you see them?"

"Nope," I lied and turned toward Carly. "Did you pass them on the road?"

She shook her head, a small tear sliding down her cheek. "I didn't see them either."

"And what about us?" Chris asked. "Did you think twice before sending *us* out in that storm? Did you wonder at all if *we* had made it safely to the reintegration facility?"

"No. Well, yes." She paused and bowed her head, blindly searching the ground for an explanation. "If I'd known there was an accident, if I'd suspected you boys hadn't made it safely to the reintegration facility, then I would've gone looking for you myself."

"Well, you're in luck, because now you don't have to," Chris replied, holding his hands out wide. "We came to you."

"What happened to the others on your van?" she asked. "Where are they?"

"We're it," Chris said.

"What do you mean, 'we're it'?'"

Chris pointed in Carly's direction. "Like the girl said, it's only the three of us. Her car slammed into our van and we rolled down the embankment. She managed to climb out of her car before it fell over the edge, smashing, yet again, into our van. If you ask me, it's all her fault. She's the one who caused the whole accident in the first place."

Carly shot Chris a glare, and I swallowed down my laughter. Chris would play along for me, but there was no way he was going to let Carly forget who it was that set all this in motion.

"Chris and I got out," I quickly said before Carly had a chance to fire something stupid back at Chris. "We checked the others, but none of them were breathing. We found Carly crawling out of her car up on the road. Like Chris said, she barely made it before her car tumbled over the ledge."

"You mean they're all dead?"

"Yep. Every single one of them," Chris shot back. "Not sure what you guys expected, though." He stepped up to the fence and curled his fingers through the links. "You shipped a van full of innocent teens out onto icy roads in the middle of a blizzard. What exactly were you hoping would happen?"

I waved Ms. Tremblay off when she went to answer. My toes were numb, my shoulder killed, and I was two steps away from falling flat on my face. I'd tell her whatever she wanted to know as soon as she let us in.

"Please, can we go inside?" I begged. "I'm tired, and cold, and everything hurts."

Ms. Tremblay hesitated for a second, then walked back

toward the door, her eyes landing squarely on me as she pounded on the steel frame. "I'm sorry," she said. "And I meant what I said. I would've come looking for you myself, had I only known."

NINETEEN

The harsh fluorescent lighting in the room seared through my eyelids, intensifying the headache threatening to split open my skull. Now that we were finally inside, warm and relatively safe, the adrenaline that had kept me moving disappeared, and I began to comprehend exactly what I had gotten myself into.

"I thought you said the storm knocked the power out," I said, fishing for information on the generators. We were sitting in a room I'd never been in before, in a part of the building I didn't even know existed. And the lights seemed to be working fine to me.

"It did," the guard who'd been assigned to us replied. "Backup generators."

"There's more than one?" I said, hoping Chris had also caught that distinction.

"There are three," Ms. Tremblay replied, not even turning to acknowledge me. She'd sent for the Bake Shop's only medic and was watching over his shoulder as he assessed Carly's injuries. Chris had a gash on his head and some nasty-looking cuts where he'd literally dug shards of glass out of his leg. I was exhausted and seriously contemplating slicing my toes off rather than dealing with the pain shooting through them as they thawed out. But as usual, Ms. Tremblay didn't seem overly concerned about us. Carly first.

She'd actually taken the time to find Carly some dry clothes, had scoured her own closet looking for something comfortable and warm for Carly to wear. Not for me and Chris. The girl whose only injuries were a dirty face and scratched-up knuckles got pampered while the two guys who'd earned their way out of that place were left sitting in their own blood.

If I dug deep enough, part of me understood Ms. Tremblay's concern. After our hike here, Carly actually looked the part of a girl who'd escaped a car crash. Her eyes were bloodshot and rimmed with tears, and she was huddled into herself, shaking. But still, a little concern focused in our direction would've been nice.

"So," Ms. Tremblay started, finally satisfied that Carly's injuries were superficial at best. "Tell me what happened again."

"Let's not," I spit out, praying Carly would keep her mouth shut. Chris had gone silent, hadn't chimed in or said a word since we'd walked through the front door. And Ms. Tremblay seemed hell-bent on launching the world's most miserable game of Twenty Questions. The three of us needed to regroup. Fast.

I turned toward Chris, trying to figure out where his mind was. "You got anything to say?"

"Nope," he said with a quick shake of his head.

"It's important that we—"

"We've already told you everything," I said, cutting Ms. Tremblay off. "We can't make it any simpler. Car smashed into van. Big cliff. Fire. Everybody dead. There, is that clearer now, or do you need me to draw you a picture?" I was half tempted to grab the pen out of the medic's hand and do it. The images of the bodies, the shattered glass, and the blood-stained seats were right there at the forefront of my mind, begging to be sketched out.

"Ah, that hurts." Carly groaned, and everybody, including me, swung our heads in her direction. The medic was cleaning the scrapes on her knuckles and, from the smell of it, straight rubbing alcohol was his preferred antiseptic.

The medic hesitated for a moment before tossing the bloodied strip of gauze into the trash, apparently deciding the wound was clean enough. Either that or her little-girl-in-pain act had actually worked. "Sorry about that," he said, "but that accident banged you up pretty good."

Chris smirked, and I kicked him beneath the table. Asshole thought this was funny.

"What?" He held his hands up in the air, feigning innocence. "I'm not allowed to feel bad for the poor little girl and her teeny weeny scrapes?"

There was a loud rap on the door. The guard opened it a crack, barely enough for him to see out, then visibly relaxed and opened it wider.

I recognized the guard who entered. He'd been assigned to our block of rooms, was the guard I'd had that little conversation with about the locks and the weather the other day.

The one who'd warned me not to try anything. Murphy. And Murphy was now back in uniform, his Taser gun in full view.

His gaze roamed over Chris and me before resting on Carly. A flash of pity crossed his eyes, a crude assumption that we'd done something vile to her.

"I'm sorry to bother you," he finally said, addressing Ms. Tremblay. "But I'm trying to straighten out the sleeping arrangements for tonight. Where, exactly, are you intending to house her?"

"In the girls' quarters," Ms. Tremblay answered, waving him away as if it were the dumbest question in the world. "Each facility has one. We're required to have a minimum of three spaces devoted to female residents. I assume, since we were evaluated last month, that we're still within compliance of that mandate."

"I'm well aware of their location," Murphy replied. "And yes, under normal circumstances, the quarters are in functioning order. But housing her there isn't feasible right now."

"Why not?"

"We have enough fuel on site to keep the generators going for three days, but even that is pushing it," he said, and I did the simple addition in my head, then glanced at the clock hanging on the wall. We were in the morning of day two, 11:00 a.m. to be exact.

"In an attempt to stretch the fuel out, we cut power to those areas currently not in use," Murphy went on. "That includes the girls' quarters."

"Then reconnect the power," Ms. Tremblay suggested.

"Absolutely," Murphy said. "And what part of the building should we take that power from? Perhaps the hall that currently houses the boys? Or maybe the keypads that secure your personal quarters from the rest of the building? Or better yet, the security camera we have on the Denton kid?"

There it was—the confirmation that Carly's brother was still in there, still alive. I'd suspected it, Chris had assured me of it, but until I heard his name pass the guard's lips, I'd wondered, or maybe even hoped, that he wasn't there.

Carly gasped and straightened up at the sound of her brother's name. She inched to the edge of her seat, away from the medic and closer to the door in an attempt to better hear the conversation. I shot her a look, one that told her to stay in character.

Ms. Tremblay sighed as she glanced at Carly, the look of pity in her eyes making me physically ill. "There's no way to draw power from somewhere else? Even for one night? Until the roads have cleared and we can move her out?"

Murphy shook his head. "Not if you want the external doors locked and the isolation cells to stay secured."

"We can't house her with the boys," Ms. Tremblay thought out loud. "It's not safe."

"Why, afraid one of us might crack and take it out on her?" Chris asked, unprompted. "You afraid I might do that? Because I got news for you. We had plenty of time alone with her outside this place and I never touched her, did I, Lucas?" He shifted his position, giving both Ms. Tremblay and the guard his back. He was up to something, and knowing him, I doubted it was good.

"Well?" Chris asked again. "Did I touch her even once?"

"No," I said, completely confused as to what he was getting at. He'd barely said three words to me since we'd entered this room, and now he was getting all worked up for absolutely no reason. "You wouldn't do that."

"Nobody is suggesting that—"

"That's exactly what you're suggesting," Chris said. "That's what you thought, what you pretty much accused us of when you first saw us outside. You think I don't see the way you're looking at me now? The way you and that medic are fawning all over her while Lucas and I sit here half dead?"

Chris was up and out of his seat, his fists balled as he walked toward Carly. He mouthed something to her, something so quiet nobody else in the room could make it out. Her eyes briefly slid to me before she gave Chris a quick nod.

"Tell them the truth," Chris demanded. "Did I hurt you? Did I ever once lay a finger on you?"

Carly hesitated, her entire body sinking into the chair she was sitting in. Her eyes caught mine and she mouthed a quick "sorry" before she turned to Ms. Tremblay and said, "No, Chris never touched me."

"Are you saying Lucas did?" Ms. Tremblay asked.

Carly brought her hands to her face, trembling like some traumatized little girl.

"What the hell are you talking about?" I stood up, knocking over the chair I was sitting in. I'd risked everything for this girl, and she was screwing it all up with some fake story about how I'd hurt her. "I never touched you. Neither of us did."

Carly was sobbing now, her tiny body shaking in time

with her whispered words as tears streamed down her cheeks. "Stop yelling at me," she hiccupped before turning to Chris. "How could you? How could you just stand there and watch him?"

Before I had a chance to even process the absurdity of what I was doing, I launched myself at her. I wanted to wrap my hands around her throat and choke the truth out of her. Accusing me of hurting her, in any way, would get me locked up forever. No going home. No seeing Suzie. No college or friends. No future. "Have you lost your mind?"

Murphy came out of nowhere and wrapped an arm around my throat, tightening it into a chokehold. I struggled against him, hurling every curse I could think of at Carly as he wrestled me face-first into the wall. I'd risked my life to save her brother, convinced Chris to do the same, and here she was, lying.

I twisted against Murphy's hold, landing an elbow to his ribs. He doubled over and groaned, letting go of me in the process. He backed up and widened his stance, bracing himself for my next move. I lowered my head and surged forward, intent on tackling him to the ground.

Light streaked across my vision. A crackling sound hovered in the air, milliseconds before a sharp pain shot through my chest and lodged itself at the base of my spine. My entire body tensed. My knees buckled and I tried to scream, but nothing came out. Nothing but a painful gasp of air. Someone lowered me to the ground, the arms around me tightening as every muscle in my body seized up.

TWENTY

I'd never been hit with a Taser before, but I knew damn well what a concentrated shot of electricity could do to your system. Knew it could leave a person shaking uncontrollably as they lost control of their muscles. And thanks to Chris and Carly, I was now sitting in a glass cage in the isolation unit, trying uselessly to still my tremors.

Chris was in the same glass room as me; Carly was in the next one over. My focus wasn't good enough to make out the shadow in the cube across from us, but if I had to hazard a guess, I'd say it was the coveted Cam Denton. And after everything that happened in the past hour, I was more likely to leave Carly's brother behind to rot than try to save him.

"What the hell just happened?" My mind realigned with my body just long enough to get those five words out, and even that took a painful amount of energy.

"Keep your voice down," Chris said, wincing as he massaged his temples. "I've got a welt on my ass the size of Texas, and my head feels like it's about to explode."

I wasn't sure if he was referring to being quasi-electrocuted or the injuries from the accident, but I got what he was saying nonetheless. "They got you too?"

He nodded. "Yep. I took a swing at Murphy. Bastard had no business tasing you."

"And what about her?" Carly was the last person I'd expected to find down here in the bowels of hell. The way they'd coddled her upstairs, I figured she'd be safely tucked away in Ms. Tremblay's room, drinking tea and eating cookies.

"She went for the second guard's gun. Of course, Ms. Tremblay tried to convince the guards that Carly only reacted out of fear and to leave her in her care, but that didn't fly."

I quickly glanced at Carly. From the looks of it, she hadn't received so much as a slap on the hand for her actions upstairs. Figures. Electrocute the boys and leave the batshit-crazy girl unharmed.

"They left you some clean clothes," Chris said, pointing to the jeans and T-shirt sitting on the cot next to him. "I'd turn my back to give you some privacy, but these walls are glass, so what I don't see, she will."

"Screw you," I said as I literally crawled my way over to the cot and pulled the clothes down to the floor next to me. Let Carly look all she wanted; it'd be the first and last look at me she got.

I pulled the shirt over my head, enjoying the feel of clean, warm clothes. It felt good to change, to sit in something that wasn't covered in vomit and dirt.

"You want to tell me what that was all about?" I asked, quite sure Chris had orchestrated the little stunt upstairs.

"Got us down here, didn't it?" Chris said, a smug smile playing across his face.

"You did this?" I asked. "You actually planned this?"

"Not *this*, exactly," he said, his hand fluttering to my half-naked state and the pile of soiled clothes sitting next to me. "But getting us down here, in plain sight of Cam, yeah ... that was my plan all along. I figured inciting the guards was the quickest way to do it. Carly playing along ... well, that was just an added bonus."

Anger set in and I didn't know who I wanted to get my hands on more, him or Carly. "When were you gonna clue me in?"

"I wasn't." Chris shrugged his apology. "You know, she never actually accused you of anything. You came to that conclusion all on your own, and it worked."

"What the hell do you mean, 'it worked'?"

"We needed you to snap, for all three of us to go after each other so that we'd get tossed down here close to Cam. And that was the first idea I came up with. If it's any consolation, the guards and Ms. Tremblay don't believe you did it either."

"Not good enough," I growled out. "Not even close."

"I don't know what to tell you," Chris started. "I agreed to help you, but I'm not gonna log any more time here than I have to. I want out of here, and you snapping was the quickest way I could think of to get us down here."

I kicked at my dirty clothes on the floor. Shit, I couldn't

deny that his messed-up plan had worked. We were now within feet of Cam.

"So that's Cam," I said, tilting my head toward the shadow of a person in the cell across from ours.

"Yup. Or what's left of him anyway. He hasn't so much as moved, didn't even raise his head when they dragged us down the stairs."

Fantastic. That was just what I wanted to hear. I'd risked my life to save someone who was pretty much gone to begin with.

My gaze shifted back to Carly. She was staring at her brother, her shoulders hunched and her entire body curled in on itself. Despite her little game upstairs, I felt bad for her. I'd been where she now was, staring at the shell of my brother, wondering what had gone wrong. Difference was, her brother might still have had a chance.

"She all right?" I didn't know why I'd asked; it wasn't like either of them deserved an ounce of my consideration.

Chris nodded and shifted his position on the bed so he could see Carly through the glass wall. "Yup. She's been watching him like that for the last hour. I don't think he's looked back once."

"So what now?" I reached down, yanked off my sneaker, and pulled the stupid flash drive from my sock. Every single piece of proof Joe had collected, the key to our freedom, was stored on that tiny stick. If I'd been smart, I would've tossed it at Ms. Tremblay through the fence and walked away, hiked the forty miles to the reintegration facility, and finished out my time in peace. But no, I had to get sucked into Carly's stupid plan to save her brother.

"Ms. Tremblay isn't going to believe a word we say, not after this." I threw the flash drive across the room, doubting it would be any use to me now. It bounced off the glass wall and landed at my feet. "Any idea how to get us out of this fish bowl?"

"Weren't you paying attention upstairs?" Chris asked.

I snorted. "No, I was too busy writhing around on the floor to listen to Ms. Tremblay's incessant ramblings."

"Well, they have enough fuel to keep this place secure for three days."

"I know that," I barked. "What else did they say?"

"We're in the middle of day two, and according to the argument upstairs, the one you missed while you were 'writhing around on the floor'"—he paused only long enough to air-quote his words—"they're trying to decide which section of the building to pull power from to secure these two additional cells we now call home."

"And..." I fanned my hands out for him to continue. Lower security was better, would make our job easier.

"They're running on the bare minimum as it is."

"Which means?"

"They're diverting power from that other section to these cells down here. Being that we're so dangerous and all," Chris said. "Using more power will cut the generators' run-time, and my guess is that the fancy locks on these doors and the cameras above our bed suck up a crap-load of power."

"Which means the time frame for the generators just

got cut way down," I reasoned, a flare of excitement building inside me. For once, something was going in my favor.

"If I'm right, which I usually am, those doors are going to unlock all on their own tomorrow morning when the generators fail. If not sooner," Chris said.

"And we're supposed to just sit here and wait until that happens?"

"Sounds good to me," Chris said as tucked his hands behind his head and lounged on the cot.

I stood up, bracing myself against the wall for support as I eased myself toward the door. I tested it, pushing the full weight of my body against the six-inch-thick glass, wishing I could just shove my way out.

"Twelve hours," Chris called out from behind me. "Give it twelve hours, and I guarantee that door will slide open all on its own."

"And then what? We grab Cam and stroll up those stairs and out the front door?" Sitting in the cell, locked up with nothing to do but wait, I began to realize just how bad our plan was. All we'd hammered out as a group was the lie we would sell to get us inside. After that, we had absolutely nothing figured out.

TWENTY-ONE

Three hours. Three miserable hours had passed since they'd dropped us into this cube, and I was already going nuts. Carly had given up staring at Cam and was now pacing in a tight circle like a caged animal. No way would that girl survive a day, never mind six weeks, in a place like this. But then again, neither had her brother.

A savage scream erupted from Carly's throat and she hurled herself at the glass wall, her fists connecting with it over and over again. Cam didn't move; he didn't so much as flinch. How he was tuning her out so completely, how he lacked even the tiniest bit of empathy for a girl obviously in so much pain, amazed me. She was one of my least favorite people in the world right then, but even I felt bad for her.

It was dead silent in our glass cell, but my mind refused to shut down. I spent most of my time staring at the circular security camera mounted on the ceiling, memorizing its schedule.

They'd turned it on when they first locked us down there, the red light constantly twitching. Since then, they'd cut it back, the camera only activating every ten minutes. And pretty soon, I guessed, even that would stop.

I glanced over at Chris, astounded that he could sleep through any of this. With each peaceful breath Chris let out, I alternated between wanting to smother him with that thin, pathetic excuse for a pillow he rested his head on and patting him on the shoulder. Somehow his ability to completely ignore things both impressed and scared the crap out of me.

"Get up," I yelled, kicking his cot with my foot. He grumbled something inaudible and rolled over, but I could tell he was awake. His breathing had changed, his body tensing as he remembered where he was.

"Just how sure are you that those doors are going to unlock?" I asked, shoving Chris's feet off the side of the cot so I could sit down.

"Positive," Chris answered, pushing himself up. "This far out in the middle of nowhere, they've gotta be fueling the generators with actual gasoline. Once all their red containers are empty, they won't be able to power anything. Why?"

"Nothing, just thinking out loud." Part of me didn't really believe the generators would run out of fuel. Our neighbors back home, the Jenkins, used to have one. They would drag it out whenever there was a storm and the power went out. Thing was as loud as hell and kept me up at night. The problem was, generators were usually kept outside, and I wasn't sure Chris slipping in and out of the Bake Shop's doors to mess with the generators—if we could even get out of these cubes—was possible.

He went to lie back down, and I put out my hand to

stop him. He may have been at ease with the sit-tight-and-wait-for-the-generators-to-fail plan, but not me. All that waiting afforded me was an excess of time to dream up all the ways things could go wrong. Deadly wrong.

"What about the lights above the doors?" I asked. I'd been running over contingency plans in my head for hours, and none of them seemed workable. "Those have their own battery backups, right?"

Chris tilted his head toward the door at the top of the stairs. There was an exit sign hanging there with a floodlight attached to each side. "Yeah, they run on batteries. Once the generators fail, they'll come on."

"For how long?" I asked.

"I don't know. At least six hours, more likely eight." He paused and looked up. There was an emergency light above each of the three glass cells, as well.

"And the chance of the actual power coming back on before then?" I asked.

Chris shrugged. "We passed at least one downed utility pole on our way here. Plus, you heard Nick—there's a transformer down, and those can take days to fix. I doubt the power will be back on anytime soon, but if you're looking for absolute certainties…" He paused and tossed his hands out, not willing to even hazard a guess.

I wasn't looking for absolutes, but something a little better than 60-40 would've put me at ease. My biggest fear was that the electric company would find a way to fix the power before we had a chance to get out of there. A facility housing a bunch of high-risk teens must have been at the top of their power-restoration list.

"If I can get you to the main electrical panel, do you think you could cut the power to this place for good?" I was hoping for a yes, but at that point, I would've settled for a strong maybe.

"Absolutely," Chris replied. "But that would require us having unmonitored movement around the facility, and I don't see that happening."

"What if we created a diversion, something that would occupy all the guards' time for a couple of hours?"

"And how the hell do you plan to do that?" Chris asked. "Everyone is upstairs, and you were against bringing Nick or anybody else in here with us. It's just you and me, buddy. I'm not sure what kind of diversion we can drum up on our own."

I was slowly beginning to regret leaving Nick and Joe outside. Having a few more of the Carly's friends in here to cause a distraction was exactly what we needed. Without them, I had to bank on the people already in here for help. Guys like me. Strangers. People who society believed were destined to become the next Charles Manson.

"We gotta get upstairs," I said, cringing at my own suggestion. "We're going to need some help distracting the guards if we have any chance of getting out of here with Cam. If we can convince even two of the other guys in here to try and escape, then it'll scatter the guards and make it easier for us to handle Cam." I glanced over at Carly's brother. From the looks of it, I doubted he would put up much of a fight or do anything more than mumble something incoherent as he slid farther into the darkness of his own mind.

"I still don't see the point in saving him," Chris muttered under his breath.

I didn't either, but I'd promised Carly I would at least try. "I need to get upstairs," I repeated. I was done waiting for the generators to run out of gas.

"*We* need to get upstairs," Chris corrected. "And do you have any idea how to accomplish that?"

I looked at the camera. "We need to catch the attention of whoever is watching that feed," I said, knowing full well that the only thing that ever got any notice around here was violent behavior.

TWENTY-TWO

"Okay. So let's go over it again," Chris said, distracting me from my attempt to catch Carly's attention. There was no way to communicate my actual plan to her, no way for me to tell her to check her emotions and follow my lead. And given her rather sketchy track record thus far, I wasn't feeling too confident in her ability to follow my non-verbal cues. "In about three minutes, that camera is going to come back on."

"Give or take a few seconds," I said, waffling my hands in the air. The surveillance times had gotten unpredictable, shifting from twelve minutes of silence, to eighteen, then back to twelve. To be honest, sixteen was nothing more than a guess.

"Got it," Chris said, waving me off. "And when it comes on, you're going to hit me, and I'm going to pretend it hurts, maybe even fall down and roll around on the floor like a pansy. Then we wait and hope one of the guards video-stalking us comes down to my rescue."

I nodded. That plan, as crappy as it was, was pretty much it. Except Chris wasn't going to have to pretend anything; I had every intention of hurting him. Call it payback for his stunt upstairs.

"Here's the thing, though," Chris said. "Being that we lived with each other in a ten-by-ten-foot room for a month and never so much as laid a finger on each other, aren't the guards going to think it's weird that when we *aren't* being subjected to psychological stress testing, we go after each other?"

"Maybe," I mumbled, not really caring either way. All I needed was a momentary distraction so one of us could slip upstairs.

"Or that we've been sitting here calmly for nearly five and half hours, and now, for absolutely no reason, you randomly lose it on me?" Chris added.

Unable to think of a rational response, I simply nodded.

"And don't forget the fact that—"

"Shut up!" I yelled. I knew my plan sucked, but that didn't mean I needed him poking more holes in it or my already shaky confidence.

He threw up his hands in a mock gesture of defeat. "I'm just saying that perhaps, considering what'll happen if we screw this up, we should take a little more time to think this through."

The time for thinking was over, and I stood up, irritated enough to put some serious force behind the fist I intended to slam into his jaw. I took a deep breath and pulled back my arm, channeling a week's worth of pent-up aggression, then got completely sidetracked by the streak of brown bouncing off the glass wall to my right.

I swore and spun around to see what the hell Carly

wanted. That girl had the worst timing ever. She'd ignored us the entire time down there, and now that I was ready to do something to get us out, she decided to launch her boot at the glass wall.

"What the hell do you want?" I yelled, knowing she couldn't hear me. The glass walls were six inches thick and soundproof.

She nodded in the direction of the door. I turned in time to see Murphy, the same effin' guard who'd tased me, walking down the stairs.

"Shit." I breathed out, distancing myself from Chris. "What's he doing here?" He wasn't supposed to show up until *after* I'd knocked Chris out.

I reached for the flash drive I'd thrown across the room earlier and stuffed it into my sock before jamming my feet back into my sneakers. The guard was standing by Carly's cell, punching something into the keypad mounted outside the door. She stepped out, her eyes meeting mine, and I shook my head. The last thing I needed was for her to make a move on him. She didn't stand a chance against the guard, and it would kill my already bad plan if she did something stupid.

"Trust me," I mouthed to Carly.

Carly stayed still, one foot still inside her glass cube, as the guard made his way toward our door. He slid it open and stepped inside our cell, his hand permanently melded to the Taser gun I was intimately familiar with.

"I'm only going to say this once," he started, his voice echoing painfully through our glass cube. "I need you to follow me upstairs. Either one of you makes a move for her, or for me, and that little shock I gave you earlier is going to seem like a walk in the park compared to what I'll do. Understand?"

"Loud and clear," I said, pushing past him.

"What's going on?" Chris asked.

"We finally got a call out to the utility company. They're working on restoring the power as we speak, but until then, we're going to house all of you in one room to conserve resources."

I felt more than saw Chris's grin. He'd heard the same note of fear in the man's voice as I had. This wasn't about conserving power; this was about consolidating their security staff, containing the risk, which in this case was us.

Murphy gestured for us to stand against the wall, his hands shaking as he fumbled with the keys to the door at the top of the stairs. My eyes instinctually traveled to the ceiling and what I knew what was happening on the main floor. They were panicking. Good. Let them be afraid. Let them feel half of what we'd been subjected to.

Chris took the steps two at a time, only to meet the warning glare of a second guard waiting for us at the top. I was only a few steps up before I realized Carly wasn't following me. She'd stopped at the edge of Cam's cell and just stood there, staring at him.

Shit, I knew she wouldn't simply leave him behind.

"Carly?" I held my hand out to her, beckoning her forward, my eyes pleading with her to trust me. To trust Chris.

"Cam," she mouthed to me, and I nodded. I was aware of the problem; I just didn't know how to solve it yet.

"What about him?" I asked Murphy, tipping my head toward Cam's cell. "Isn't he coming up with us?"

"Nope." He flicked the light switches off until only the small bulb illuminating Cam's cell was on. Cam flinched. It was the first time I'd seen him move. Although I'm not sure you could call wrapping your hands around your knees and rocking in place purposeful movement ... more like a change from one broken state to another.

Carly saw it too, and her face fell as she watched her brother slip deeper into himself.

"The guard up there is going to escort the three of you to the common area, where the others are being housed," Murphy said, again gesturing for us to go up the stairs.

"But when the power goes out—" Carly started to say, and I cut her off with a wave of my hand. She needed to shut up and remember that as far as the guards were concerned, she had no connection to Cam. None at all.

But in true Carly fashion, she didn't listen. "You can't leave him down here. Alone."

"He's been down here alone for weeks," Murphy responded. "It's the safest place for him."

TWENTY-THREE

The room they shoved us into was cramped. Thirteen of us, plus five guards, the medic, and Ms. Tremblay, all housed in what looked like the staff lounge. There were a few scattered chairs, a couch, a small refrigerator, and a flat-screen TV I was quite sure wouldn't work.

The boys were spaced out, scattered across the room, most of them huddled into groups of two or three. They didn't look like they'd been intentionally arranged that way; more likely they'd done it themselves. Buddy up and pick your allies wisely. It was a fact of life in this place, one Chris and I had sworn by.

Every single head swung in our direction. Carly moved closer to me, her sideways step almost unperceivable. But Ms. Tremblay caught it and rose from her perch in the corner, her smile genuine as she made her way over to Carly.

"There are lot of adults in here. I promise that you'll be safe," she said, trying to coax Carly farther into the room.

Carly looked from one boy to the next, then back to me, an unspoken plea to protect her swirling in her eyes. She may not have grasped it before, but judging by the fear I could feel pouring off of her, she did now.

I reached out and grabbed her hand, tentatively taking it in mine, waiting for her reaction. She hadn't exactly been predictable so far, and I wasn't sure if she would trust me or throw me under the bus. It took her a second, but eventually she squeezed back, rotating her hand and lacing her fingers through mine.

A stunned silence swept over Ms. Tremblay as she stared at our intertwined hands. For once, the woman had absolutely nothing to say.

I kicked the heel of Chris's shoe. He'd been too focused on taking stock of the room to have caught Carly's initial flair of panic. A quick glance at her hand tucked into mine was all the hint he needed. "She's with us," he declared as he slid in front of Carly, blocking everyone's view of her.

Ms. Tremblay went to move around him, but he matched her step for step. Giving up, she simply held out her hand, beckoning Carly forward. There was maybe an inch between me and Carly, but Carly closed it quickly, angling her body behind mine—a clear sign that she trusted me and nobody else. *Finally.*

"Like I said," Chris repeated. "She's with us."

A thousand thoughts flew across Ms. Tremblay's face, suspicion finally setting in. Carly's switch from scared victim to friend made absolutely no sense to her.

I slid my hand free of Carly's and moved it to the small of her back, positioning her between me and Chris. I doubted any of the guys in here would touch her, but I wasn't taking any chances.

We took a communal step farther into the room, and I scanned their faces, looking for someone familiar. My eyes traveled downward, stopping at their feet. "Shoes," I whispered to Chris. They were all wearing their facility-issued jeans and white T-shirts, but their sneakers and socks had been removed.

"Guards must be freaked if they're worried about them using their Nikes as weapons," Chris replied.

The guard who'd escorted us up here caught Chris's remark. "Shoes and socks," he demanded, holding out his hand.

I curled my toes around the flash drive. I needed to keep my shoes on, at least until I had a chance to get Ms. Tremblay alone. "If it's all the same to you, I'd like to keep them. My feet have barely begun to thaw out as it is."

The guard went to argue, but the medic cut him off. "For Christ's sakes, Charles. Let them keep their shoes. In fact, did they ever get the heating pads and soup I asked you to bring them?"

The guard shook his head and took a seat. Not that I cared about his lapse in judgment. The fear and anger coursing through my system had kept me plenty warm.

"One guard at the door, one in each corner," Chris whispered as we lowered ourselves to the ground by the far wall. Knowing Chris, he'd purposefully picked this spot—it gave him a clear view of the door and everybody in the room.

"Thirteen of us," I said, counting again. "Almost two to one against the adults. I like those odds."

"Fourteen of us, if you count Cam," Carly added.

I caught the haunted hope in her voice, the distant belief that somehow, someway, Cam would magically snap out of it and be the same brother she remembered. He wouldn't. I'd stake my life on that.

"You know that even if we manage to get him out, he won't be the same person you remember," I told her gently. "The Cam you knew is gone, Carly. Probably for good."

She didn't disagree, just asked, "Was Tyler like that? When he first came home, did he act like that? Like he wasn't even really there?"

Tyler may have been distant and closed off, but he was still "there." He talked to Olivia, wrote his thoughts down in his journal, would even give you a non-verbal answer if you asked him a question. He'd only technically lost it once.

On his third day home, he'd spent every waking minute staring out his bedroom window. Mom asked him if he wanted to go outside, maybe light the grill for dinner or sit in the back-yard and get some fresh air. He flipped out on her and tore his room apart, destroying everything. Olivia finally got him to calm down, even convinced him to tell her what had set him off. According to her, it was the open space and the fresh air that had scared the shit out of him. He needed four tight walls and darkness, needed the sensation of a cage to feel safe.

But Cam … yeah, Tyler had nothing on Cam.

"Tyler was different when he came home." It was the truth, a watered-down version of it, but the truth all the same. Anything more might upset her, and what I needed right now was for Carly to stay strong and follow my lead.

"You think Cam will kill himself too?" Carly asked, and I wondered if she was regretting coming here, if the small glimpse she'd gotten of her brother had her questioning whether or not any of this was even worth it.

"No," I lied. He would; he absolutely would. I'd contemplated it myself once or twice these past few weeks, and according to their tests, I was mentally sound.

"Maybe once he's home, maybe once he sees his friends and Mom and Dad, things will go back to normal. He'll get better. He has a girlfriend, you know. I know Olivia couldn't help Tyler, but maybe it will be different with Cam."

"Maybe," I said, selfishly not wanting to destroy whatever determination she had left. Carly needed to commit to the plan, hard and fast, or it was her life and not Cam's that would be in danger.

Chris leaned over Carly and tapped me on the shoulder. "I don't recognize any of them, do you?"

I took another quick look around the room, then shrugged. "Nope, but it's not like we were allowed to associate with anybody outside our little group. Everybody I would've recognized is lying dead in that van."

Chris sighed, a heavy sound that told me his mind was traveling the same disturbing path as mine. There was no one left here that we knew, no one we could guarantee would take our side. "You got any idea who to approach first?"

I shook my head. No matter how you sliced it, it was a crapshoot. Where one guy might jump at the chance to escape, another might run to Ms. Tremblay or the guards, hoping to score brownie points. I pointed to the guy directly across from us. He'd been fidgeting since we got in there, his gaze darting between us and the door. He was either scared of Chris and me or was trying to come up with a way out. Whichever it was, I figured he was as good of a place to start as any.

"Him," I said. "I say we start with him."

TWENTY-FOUR

"Not the best way to spend your day, huh?" I said, taking a seat on the floor next to fidgety-kid. He was alone. As cramped as this room felt, he'd managed to carve out an island for himself. "I'm Lucas, by the way."

He nodded, not offering his name or taking the hand I'd extended in his direction.

"That's Chris, and her name is Carly," I continued, and his eyes drifted up, sweeping over both of them before settling back on the tile floor.

I sat there for a minute, watching as he traced the outline of the tiles with his foot, questioning my decision to choose this particular guy. But there was something about him that I liked, that I could relate to. Maybe it was the way he kept to himself, or the fact that he hadn't bothered to ask my name. Stick to yourself. Mind what you do and what you say. You're not here to make friends; just survive and get out. That had been my plan when I first got here. His too, I imagined.

"You have a name?" I asked.

"I do," he mumbled, again not offering it up.

I laughed. He was good. Better than me.

"I've been in this place for thirty days," I said, leaving out my brief stint on the outside. I needed him to talk. I needed to find some common ground I could use to gain his trust. "How long have you been here?"

"Eight days," he mumbled, looking up at the clock attached to the wall. "Eight days, nine hours, and twenty-six minutes."

"Which one is your roommate?" I asked. We all had roommates; that was part of the testing protocol. Cramped quarters, sweltering hot temperatures, and an overload of adrenaline to toss at each other. It was like forced interaction under the most extreme of circumstances.

He jutted his chin in the direction of the lone reclining chair. A guy who easily weighed two-fifty was sprawled out in it, napping. If that'd been my roommate, I'd have left him alone too.

"I'd like to say it gets easier, that the first week is the hardest, but that'd be a lie," I said.

"How do you know that?" he asked.

"Been there, done that." I replied. "My only advice is to make sure you have the bottom bunk. It won't make any difference until about the third week in, but trust me, having a body above you to block the view will save your sanity."

"Okay," he said, not asking me to explain.

"You see that girl over there, the one I walked in with?" I was banking everything on the hope that I'd picked the right guy. "She doesn't belong in here, and I need to get her out."

"Then what's she doing here?" he asked.

"They were moving us to the reintegration facility," I started, launching into our well-rehearsed story. "The weather was bad and there was an accident. We hit her car head-on. Chris and I were the only ones in our van who survived. We found her on the road, dazed and confused," I continued, skirting the truth.

"And you brought her here?" Was that disbelief or judgement I heard in his voice? Either way, it made me like him a little bit more.

"This was the closest shelter I knew of. Besides, it's not like the weather was cooperating with us."

He cocked his head as if he wasn't buying my answer, and I quickly changed my approach rather than risk losing him altogether. "It doesn't matter why or how she got here, just that she is. The roads are closed, and they pretty much said they won't be able to get her out for a few days. But you saw the way the guards looked at her when we first walked in. I'm not sure she'd survive a night, never mind a few days, in here."

He shrugged, as if to say *not my problem*.

It wasn't, but I was about to make it his problem all the same.

"Ever thought about what it would be like to walk out of here? To go back home and put all this behind you? Start over?" I felt like crap baiting him, but if he wouldn't consider helping Carly, if he wouldn't sacrifice anything without a little incentive, then so be it.

He looked up, unable to hide his interest. "You think it's possible?"

"I know it is. Why do you think we're all sitting here in this staff lounge instead of locked up nice and tight in our rooms?"

I leaned back and watched him as he tossed my words around in his mind. Twice he opened his mouth to speak, and twice he snapped it shut, his eyes darkening and his breath catching in his throat.

"It's a test," he said without a hitch. "They want to see how we interact in a larger group, see who goes for who first."

I shook my head. That had Ms. Tremblay written all over it; convince them this was some sort of evaluation they had to pass to keep them in line.

"The power to the building is out," I said. "There's a transformer down about ten miles south of here. Even after they get that up, they have about a dozen other smaller utility poles to fix."

"How do you know that?"

"Van. Crash. Long walk back here with that girl," I said, refreshing his memory. "In a few hours, the generators powering this place are going to cut out, and the only thing that will be separating you … separating us all from the outside is them. No locks, no electrified fences, nothing."

"Thirteen against five," he mumbled, and I found it interesting that he completely discounted the medic and Ms. Tremblay from the equation. It was as if he knew they were unarmed and posed no threat.

"Exactly," I said, nearly positive he was coming around to my idea. "Easy pickings."

He pointed to the guard who'd escorted us up to this room. "I want that one."

I laughed but didn't argue. I briefly wondered what that guard had done to him, what sort of special attention he'd directed the kid's way. In the end, I didn't care which guard he claimed for himself, so long as he caused one hell of a distraction in the process. "He's all yours, buddy. But do me a favor and give him an extra shove for me."

I stood up, my eyes already scanning the room for my next recruit. One on our side was good, but I'd feel better with a few more at our back. My focus settled on the three guys sitting near Chris. They were all playing cards, but one had his cards face-down on the floor as if he'd bowed out after the first deal.

"Not that one," fidgety-kid said. "If you're looking for more of us to help, then I would steer clear of him. Ask them." I followed his gaze to the corner, where two identical-looking boys sat staring at each other. Twins. Smart choice; brothers would do almost anything for each other. I should know. I would've laid down my life right then for Tyler had I been given the chance.

"And my name's Ryan by the way," he added. "Ryan Banks."

TWENTY-FIVE

Thanks to Ryan, I recruited the twins with ease and moved on to take my chances with a couple of exhausted-looking guys at the other end of the room. I remembered that feeling of being totally spent—the alarms, the lights, and the constant need to be on high alert. I hoped they were in better physical shape than they were mentally, that the fear and exhaustion in their faces was nothing compared to the desperation in their minds. But then again, it didn't much matter. It wasn't an all-out brawl I was looking for, just time.

"Five guys," I said as I sank to the ground next to Chris. "Is five enough, or do you think we need more?"

"I don't know about this," Carly whispered. I'd let Chris explain the finer details of our plan to her while I took on recruitment duty. "We're going to sit here and wait for the generators to go out, and then hope those five can create enough of a distraction to occupy the guards? Pray that we don't get caught up in the chaos and can slip out unnoticed?"

I nodded. Unfortunately, that sounded about right.

"And then Chris is somehow going to cut the power to the main circuit board while you and I go for Cam," she finished.

"I have to get Joe's files to Ms. Tremblay too, don't forget that," I added, quite sure Carly cared more about getting her brother out than anything else.

"Sure, the files," Carly said, dismissing the idea. "And the guys you talked to, you're positive they'll help?"

"We have no choice but to trust them," I replied. "The guards aren't exactly on our side, and while Joe may trust Ms. Tremblay, I sure as hell don't."

"So we're going to leave them all here to fend for themselves while we go get Cam?"

"Umm hmm." The look of disappointment on Carly's face hit me in the gut. I didn't know what she expected me to say. I'd come back to save her brother. As for the rest of them, that's where Joe's research would come into play. "I can't exactly save them *and* help you get to Cam at the same time. Pick your poison."

"This all sucks," she said.

"Sucks is pretty much the way things work around here," Chris said.

————

The lights flickered twice, then dimmed, as if the generators had turned everything down five notches in a futile attempt to keep working. The five people clued in on our plan tensed, their eyes swinging in my direction, silently asking what to do. I grabbed ahold of Chris's arm, my signal for them to sit tight.

One of the guards handed Ms. Tremblay a Taser gun. She balanced it in her hand, testing the weight. She looked confused, as if she had no idea how to use it. It seemed pretty simple to me. All you had to do was point and pull the trigger; the electrical current did the rest.

I'd have given anything to get my hands on one of those. Not for protection, but because I'd love to light up Murphy, let him wallow in a puddle of his own misery for a change.

"Do you have any idea where the main electrical panel might be?" I asked Chris, my mind running through details we should've long since figured out.

He shook his head. "Nope, but my guess is in the basement, most likely on an outer wall. How hard can it be to find?"

Given the size of that place, pretty hard. But voicing that would've only put unnecessary credence behind my fears. "What about the guard who's still downstairs with Cam?" I asked, wondering how Chris planned to slip into the lower level of the facility unnoticed.

"I doubt that's the only entrance to the basement," Chris replied, unconcerned. "This place is huge, and it doesn't make sense that they'd house the mechanical equipment next to the isolation unit."

"And you'll meet us down there by Cam," I said, seeking out his assurance. I was positive I'd have to carry Cam out of there, and I wanted Chris's help if it came to that. Or at least a spare set of hands to fend off anybody who tried to stop me.

"Yep, that's the plan. Staircase by the door to the isolation unit," he said, then leaned toward Carly. "Remember what I said. Stay close to Lucas and do what he says."

"It's about to get dark in here fast," I said, just to remind Carly. "People aren't going to take the time to figure out who you are before they throw a punch. I know for a fact most of these guys want out, and they'll go through you to get there. So no matter what happens, stay close to me."

The lights flickered again, and the guards spread out, moving away from the walls, crowding us in. They looked hesitant, scared, and I couldn't help but laugh. What was it my old English teacher used to say? Some random crap about the hunter becoming the prey? That's how it was, and I had a distinct feeling they knew it.

There was an audible click as the heat vents in the ceiling shut off, seconds before the lights. Steeped in darkness, the entire room went eerily silent. But I didn't need light or sound to know each guard had his hands on his Taser, their eyes trained on the emergency lights above the door as they waited for that tiny flare of light to come on.

"It'll take a minute or so for the emergency lights to kick in," Chris reminded me. I started ticking off the seconds in my head, willing myself to stay put and wait until the timing was just right. I rapped my hand on the wall behind my head, signaling for the five guys I'd recruited to spread out across the room and slowly count to fifty before striking together. Each one had been instructed to go for the guards in the corners. Ryan, the one I trusted the most, was covering the guard stationed by the door, the one he'd all but insisted on taking down himself.

"Forty-two. Forty-three. Forty-four." Carly was counting next to me, her nails digging into my arm with each passing second. Just as she hit fifty, the room exploded, the five guys I'd spent no more than fifteen minutes talking to risking everything for me. For a chance at a life not defined by this place or the gene they carried.

TWENTY-SIX

Luck wasn't something I flirted with, but I got it in spades that day. No one bailed on me, and luckily, no one took it upon themselves to change the plan. Chris had less than thirty seconds to smash the bulbs on the emergency light above the door. Without the cover of complete darkness and the fear it induced, we didn't have a chance.

Not trusting anybody else, Chris and I slid our way across the wall toward the door where the emergency light was threatening to come on.

I dropped down on all fours and tapped Chris's foot. He needed to move quickly and with a steady hand. He was heavier than I thought, and I forced down a grunt of discomfort as all his weight pressed into my back. He moved from side to side, his heel digging into my tailbone as he blindly swiped at the wall above his head. "Found it," he said, and in seconds his fist slammed into the light, sending shards of glass raining down around me.

"Shit," he swore as he jumped off my back. I didn't need

a light to know he was cradling his hand, carefully picking out the tiny pieces of glass embedded in his fist.

"Stairs," he said, instructing Carly to head straight for the door and wait for us outside. Without lights, the guys had a better chance of hitting one of us than a guard. And neither Chris nor I wanted Carly in the middle of that.

"You're right behind me?" she asked, her voice hesitant, untrusting.

I reached out, my hand trailing down her arm until I found her hand. I squeezed it in reassurance. Chris and I needed a few minutes to adequately stir the pot in here, and then we were out of this room: Chris headed downstairs to look for the electrical panel, and me headed for Carly and Cam.

I sensed more than saw the guys moving, heard their rage-filled screams as they charged headlong into the guards. I wondered what the rest of the group would do, the ones who had no idea that this rebellion had been staged.

The guards' guns flared to life, the flickering blue hue giving away their locations as the sound of electricity crackled through the air. They were shooting blind, training their Tasers on any and every sound in a futile attempt to regain control. One Taser made contact, and the blood-curdling scream echoing off the walls kicked me into action. I gave a not-so-gentle nudge to Chris's arm and we both took off, each of us zoning in on one blue flare. One guard.

We hit them from behind, tackling them to the ground. Mine went down with a grunt, his gun skittering across the floor. I didn't know who picked it up; all I knew was that they didn't use it on me, and for that, I was thankful.

"Shit, get off me." With nothing but the sound of his voice to guide my feet, I turned, praying Chris would say something else so I could find him and help fight off whoever was on him. No matter which way I turned, strangled curses filled the air, one coming on the heels of another until I could barely hear myself think, never mind isolate Chris's voice. My only hope was that Carly was far away before what was supposed to be a coordinated attack descended into madness.

Someone hit me from behind. There wasn't much force to it, barely enough to knock me off balance. Whoever had thrown the punch was swinging randomly, a defensive move more than anything else. It pissed me off nonetheless, and I turned around and clocked the person, spilling them to the floor.

I went to hit them again, my anger finally having an outlet and loving every second of it. It was the small whimper of a plea, a female whisper, that had me backing off.

"Please," Ms. Tremblay begged. It was one word. One simple yet insanely complicated word. This was the woman who'd spent weeks watching the guards dissect my moods and pummel my willpower. She'd stood there that entire time with her rehearsed smile and fake reassurances that "we'd all be stronger because of this experience." And now she was on the floor at my feet, pleading for mercy.

I quickly patted her down, looking for the Taser the guard had given her earlier. Her fingers were clawed around it like it was the one thing that would keep her alive. Swallowing down the urge to give her a small taste of what we'd suffered through, I ripped it from her hands and tucked it into the waistband of my jeans. In my mind, using it on her—using it on anybody—would make me no better than them.

She reached up and grabbed onto my leg, anchoring herself to me. I pulled back my other foot and was about to slam it down on her wrist to break the contact when her trembling voice broke through my concentration.

"What's happening?" Her voice seemed so tiny, so fragile compared to the explosions of unleashed anger surrounding us. "You said you could control them here, that bringing them all together was the safest option."

Ha! She assumed I was one of the guards, and that I was here to protect her. Her bad.

I went to shake her off, completely content to let her die in here until she said, "The girl ... Carly. You have to get her out of here."

Reaching down, I yanked Ms. Tremblay to her feet. Her plea to save Carly, her need to protect a girl she correctly assumed couldn't handle this place, had just saved her life. Well, that and the stupid flash drive wedged between my toes.

I grabbed her wrist and swiped my other hand out to my left, clearing a path toward what I thought was the door. My bearings were off. The noise, the flare of Tasers, and the darkness had me all turned around.

I tripped over a body, and my mind instantly flashed back to the crash, to the eight dead kids I'd left on my van. Eight dead kids whose only crime was testing positive for a gene that might, at some undetermined point in their future, make them predisposed to violence. Eight kids exactly like me and Chris. Exactly like the ones in here.

Ms. Tremblay yelped when I flattened her face-first to the wall and pressed myself into her back. I'd done this. In some stupid attempt to protect Suzie from a fate that most likely she'd never meet and get Cam out, I'd set this entire shitstorm into motion. And now here I was, determined to get the one person I despised most in this place out of this room unharmed.

I inched us along the wall, my hands at either side of her head. The wall jutted outward, a three-inch strip of metal meeting my palm. Finally, the doorjamb.

"Go back to your room and lock yourself in," I said as I guided Ms. Tremblay's hand to the doorknob. "Don't open the door for anybody, not even the guards. Understand?"

"Lucas?" she said.

I smiled at the surprise I heard in her voice. *Yes, Ms. Tremblay, even the genetically flawed are capable of being good, decent people.*

"That girl you came in with—"

"I got Carly," I promised as I opened the door and shoved her out.

Chris yelled something from behind me, his words lost in the madness overtaking the room. I heard the crack of a fist hitting someone's jaw, the body landing at my feet. "Watch your back," Chris whispered into my ear. "I'm outta here. Get moving, find Carly. Now!"

TWENTY-SEVEN

The Bake Shop really was nothing more than two floors of cinderblock-encased steel. Not only were there no exterior windows, but there were no skylights. Even the doors were made of solid metal. Essentially, the building was a cold, dark cave of interlocking corridors, all frustratingly similar. There were more rooms than I could count, and the corridors were laid out like a maze, spidering off each other. None of them looked even vaguely familiar.

The emergency lighting would have been my enemy inside the staff lounge; but, out in the hallway, I was grateful for it. It would save me minutes of precious time.

I started retracing my footsteps back to the door that led to the isolation unit, my hand trailing along the wall for extra support. I had limited time to find my way back there and meet Carly. I didn't know if it was fear, sheer exhaustion, or the punch I'd taken to the chest inside the lounge, but I suddenly felt weak and short of breath.

Rounding a corner, I stepped back and scanned the corridor for confirmation. The emergency lighting was evenly spaced—two spotlights every ten feet, all lit and guiding my way. Yet the corridor I'd just turned down, the one I was positive led to the isolation unit door, was dark. Pitch black.

Luckily, when the guard had escorted us up to the staff lounge, I'd purposefully counted my steps, memorized each turn. And as far as my calculations went, I was right where I needed to be.

So it didn't make sense. None of this made sense.

I took a tentative step down the dark corridor, paranoia quickly settling in. Maybe my gait was off, or my steps had gotten smaller once exhaustion set in. Maybe I'd miscounted or taken a wrong turn.

My foot landed on something sharp. Whatever it was jabbed through the rubber sole of my sneaker, piercing my skin. I bent down and carefully swiped my hand across the floor, wincing as shards of glass dug into my fingers. Instinctively, I looked up. There was an emergency light above my head—or at least there used to be. Now, it was nothing more than a pile of shattered glass at my feet. I was absolutely in the right hall; I was just being screwed with.

"Carly," I whispered as I inched forward, my hand making contact with what I'd assumed was the door to the isolation unit. The hall was so silent that my own breathing roared in my ears. If she was there, I couldn't hear her.

I leaned against the door, listening for a creak on the stairs, the click of an air cartridge attaching to the barrel of a Taser, the twist of the doorknob that separated me from the guard down below. Something … anything … to clue me in to what was going on.

"Where are you?" I called out into silence. This was our meeting point. This was where she was supposed to be!

"Carly!" I called out one last time, the familiar sting of fear suffocating me. I'd all but promised Nick I'd keep her safe, and already I'd lost her.

I turned around and ran back down the dark hall, the faint glow of an emergency light in the distance guiding my feet. If she wasn't at our meeting point, then chances were she was still inside the staff lounge, being beaten to death by a mob I'd purposefully incited. And I'd left her there, stupidly assuming she would follow my directions this time around.

The door to the room came into view and I paused, reeling at the sounds I could hear filtering out. Grunts of pain mingled with muted thuds filled me with terror and guilt. Crap, what had I done?

"Carly!" I yelled and ran toward the door, skidding to a halt a few inches away. I couldn't isolate a single voice, didn't know if the shrieks were coming from the guards or the kids or, worse, Carly.

A flash of blue spilled out from underneath the door, the burst of light disappearing almost instantly. A second flash lit up the small crack, quickly followed by a third and a forth. Some of the guards were still in possession of their weapons, still fighting. Either that or we had them and were firing at anything that moved.

I felt around the back waistband of my jeans for the Taser I'd gotten off Ms. Tremblay. It was gone—my hand brushed across nothing but the top of my boxers. I swore long and hard, pissed that I'd lost the only weapon any of us had managed to score.

A scream shattered my thoughts, and as I ran my hand across the doorknob, I winced in pain. Someone had wedged a shard of glass into the keyhole, jamming the lock in place. Glass littered the floor below. It was spread out in rows, waiting to meet someone's bare feet. I didn't bother to look up. I knew the emergency light above this door was functioning; it had guided me back here. Which meant the shards of glass on the floor had been placed there, purposefully picked up from a different location and dumped there *after* I'd left.

"Shit." My mind ping-ponged between opening the door to the lounge and simply finding the nearest exterior door and running for my life. Problem was, I had no clue where the exits were. That, and I couldn't leave Chris or Carly behind.

I kicked the glass as far away from the door as I could. If the kids behind that door managed to get out, then I wanted them to have at least a fighting chance, and stepping barefoot into a pile of glass would make that impossible. Every curse word I knew tumbled from my lips as I gripped the shard of glass jammed in the keyhole. It tore through my skin, and I pulled back, blood streaming from my palm. I couldn't get it to budge, not without severing my hand in half.

I put my ear to the door and tried to block everything out, listening solely for the sound of Carly's voice. I'd done the one thing I feared the most: I'd gotten her trapped in this place. I pounded my fists into the door over and over as I screamed out her name. I needed her to know I was here, that I hadn't left her. That she wasn't alone.

"What the hell are you doing?"

I spun around at the sound of Chris's voice, my eyes automatically trailing to his hands. They were bleeding, rivulets of red trickling between his fingers. "What happened to your hands?" I asked.

"I smashed the lights inside the lounge," he said, studying me as if I'd lost my mind. "What happened to yours?"

I pointed to the door and the shard of glass jammed in the lock. "I need to get back in there!"

Chris backed up, his eyes scanning the entire length of my body. "You all right?" he asked.

"I'm fine," I ground out, irritated that he was looking at me like I was completely insane.

He tore a strip of fabric off the bottom of his shirt and reached for my hand, wrapping the fabric around the gash. "You sure you're okay?" he asked again.

"I said I'm fine. Now help me with the damn door."

"Umm, okay," he said, making no move to help me. "But why do you want to go back in there? Why aren't you with Carly?"

"She's not there," I spat out, then set about trying to pick the piece of glass out of myself. "And what the hell are you doing here anyway? Aren't you supposed to be permanently taking care of the lights?"

I didn't have a watch, but even so, I knew it should've taken him much longer than five minutes to locate the electrical panel. This facility was huge. There was no way he could've found the panel, screwed with it, *and* made it all the way back up here already. No way.

"Lights are all set, and it was a hell of a lot easier getting there than back," Chris said, tilting his head toward the darkened hallway. "Thanks for that, by the way. I was unaware that smashing *all* the lights in the hallway was part of our plan. That should make it *so* much easier to find our way out."

"I didn't smash anything," I fired back. "I'm not the one with the blood dripping from my hands."

"Yeah, you are," he said, jabbing his finger at my bandaged hand. "And again, I smashed the light *inside* that room. I was standing on your back when I did it. What the hell is wrong with you, Lucas? Did you take a fist to the head or something while you were in there?"

"Well, it sure as hell wasn't me, and Carly is locked in that room, so ... "

"What are you talking about? I was just standing outside the isolation unit door talking to her," Chris said. "Why do you think I came back here looking for you? Girl's hysterical, going on about how you never made it out of the lounge."

I shook my head, not believing a word he was saying. I'd just come from our meeting spot, called Carly's name multiple times while blindly searching the hallway. She hadn't been there. Nobody was. That hallway had been empty. Dark and disturbingly empty.

TWENTY-EIGHT

I took off running, the darkness forcing me to slow my pace to a crawl as I searched my way along the cinderblock wall. Irritated that I couldn't see jack shit, I gave up and simply yelled out her name.

"Here!" Carly called back. Her voice became my guiding point, and I instructed her to keep talking, keep drawing me toward her until I eventually felt her hands closing around mine.

"Where the hell were you?" I asked, my voice rising as I struggled with the overwhelming sense of relief flooding my system. She was here, safe and standing right in front of me. "I called out to you, searched this entire hall for you, but you weren't here."

Carly squeezed my hand, and I pulled away, fought through the darkness to see her eyes.

"I was here, waiting for you and Chris the whole time." She sounded like she was out of breath, her words clipped and lodged in her throat. "You never came. I didn't know what to do or where to go."

I knew I'd followed the right halls, and she hadn't been here the first time. "No, I was here," I told her. "I came looking for you like I promised I would, but you weren't here. Nobody was."

"This is where I found her," Chris said. "She was sitting with her back to the wall, crying."

I shook my head, the events of the past few minutes becoming hazier by the second. This place could mess with your mind; that's what it was designed to do. And given Tyler's history...

"You probably took a wrong turn or something," Chris continued, as if sensing my fear. "This place is like a damn maze."

"That's not possible." Even I caught the hitch in my voice. Sure, getting turned around in the dark was plausible, but I'd counted my steps, made sure I knew exactly which way I was going. "Are you positive?" I asked Carly. "I mean, I know I was here. Right here. In this exact spot."

"Doesn't matter," Chris said. "We're all here now, so let's grab Cam, leave the flash drive in his cell, and get the hell out of here before things get any worse."

I ignored Chris and reiterated my question to Carly. "Are you sure you were here? Right here? The whole time?"

"Yes. I came straight here like you told me to. But when you didn't show up and everything went dark, I..." She trailed off.

Those emergency lights hadn't simply gone out. They were purposefully broken, including the ones in that hall, and the one directly above Carly's head. I pushed that thought to the back of my mind, unnerved by the way her voice trembled in time with her words. She must've been scared to death locked inside this building, knowing what they'd done to her brother, seeing the chaos in that room. Thinking back on it, I kicked myself for not putting the flash drive in Ms. Tremblay's hand when I took her Taser, then grabbing Carly and running. The hell with shutting this place down. The hell with Cam.

I reached out to calm Carly's fears, my hand brushing across the sleeve of her shirt. It was wet, warm, and the first thing I thought of was blood. "Are you hurt?"

"No, I'm okay," she said, flinching me off.

I didn't believe her. I'd dealt with enough blood those past two days to know what I was feeling. "No, you're not. You're bleeding."

"It's not mine." The words tumbled from her lips so fast that I almost didn't understand them. "I made it out of the lounge, but then somebody pulled me back and hit me. I clawed at them until they let me go. I couldn't see anything, so I don't know who it was. But it's their blood, not mine."

That did little to calm my rage, and I slammed my fist into the wall. This insane idea that any of us could slip in and out of this place alive was idiotic. I should've listened to my instincts and told Joe to go screw himself.

"This is so not worth it," I mumbled under my breath.

"Like I said, it doesn't matter now." Chris wrapped his palm around my fist as I went to slam it into the wall again. "Let's just finish what we started. Carly, did you happen to see who smashed the lights out here in the hall?"

"No. I didn't see anyone until you showed up. Why?"

"Because you were the only one in the hall when the light above the door to the isolation cells was knocked out. So the way I figure it, you must have seen who did it."

"I didn't see anything," Carly said. "I heard footsteps coming. At first I thought it was Lucas, but the voice was off, so I—"

"So he was talking," I interrupted. "Was it a guard or one of the guys from that room? What were they saying?"

"I don't know," Carly replied. "The only people I've ever talked to in here are the medic and Ms. Tremblay."

"And the guard in that room with us when we first got here, and the one down in the isolation unit. Also the one who escorted us to the staff room," Chris added.

"Was it any of them?" I put in. "Think Carly, was it any of them?" My eyes shifted toward the door. As far as I knew, there was only one guard *not* locked in the staff lounge, and he was sitting directly below us.

"I don't know," she said. "I honestly don't know."

I knew asking her to pinpoint the voice was useless. Without the experience with the guards that Chris and I had, she had no way of telling them apart. "Okay, forget the voice. Can you tell me what he said?"

"I wasn't paying attention to what he was saying," she replied. "I was scared and looking for you."

"And you're sure nobody followed you out of the staff lounge?" Chris asked. I remembered the brief flash of light as she'd opened the door, but I hadn't taken the time to watch her leave and make sure nobody followed her. That said, I had no idea if anybody had followed Ms. Tremblay out either. Or me or Chris for that matter.

"I'm positive no one followed me out. I waited at the door for a few seconds before I made my way here." She reached for my hand, squeezing it gently. "I was hoping you were right behind me."

"And you're convinced the guy you heard didn't see you?" Chris asked.

"I'm positive. I opened the basement door and hid on the top step until he was gone. When I came up, it was completely dark. All the lights were out and the hallway was empty."

"It had to be the guard who's watching over Cam," Chris reasoned. "I mean, who else could it be?""

"Ms. Tremblay." I regretted the words the second they left my mouth. The counselor might have been the only other person to escape the lounge as far as I knew, and god knew I hated her more than life itself most of the time, but, after hearing her beg me to keep Carly safe, I doubted she'd had a hand in any of this.

"How did she get out of the staff room?" Chris asked. "Last I checked, she was curled up in the corner clutching her precious Taser."

"She doesn't have a Taser anymore." It was a stupid reply, and one that didn't even begin to answer the question he'd asked, but somehow I thought it would help. One less person to think of as a threat. "I took it off her."

"Let me have it," Chris said.

"I don't have it. I must've dropped it fighting my way out."

"Is this it?" Carly's hand brushed mine, turning my palm

over so she could lay the Taser in my hand. I couldn't see much in the dark, but judging from the cords falling between my fingers, I knew this wasn't the same one. This gun had been fired; the probes were dangling limply from the cartridge. Ms. Tremblay's hadn't been fired.

"Where did you find this?" I asked.

"It was lying right here by the doorway. Why? Isn't it hers?"

"Yup, it's hers," I lied, and then handed it over to Chris.

TWENTY-NINE

My hand tensed on the doorknob to the isolation unit, a thousand thoughts flying through my mind all at once. None of them good. None of them even remotely helpful. We didn't have a contingency plan that included a guard stalking us or smashed emergency lights. In fact, we didn't have a contingency plan at all.

"You positive not a single light in this place is going to come back on?" I asked Chris. I needed everything from here on out to go as smoothly as possible. No more surprises. One more snag in our plan, and I'd give up altogether.

"Yup. It's not coming back on without the help of an electrical crew and a few spools of wire, trust me." Chris laughed. "I may have messed with a bit more than the circuit boards."

I tucked my hand behind me, seeking out Carly. I knew she was there, standing between Chris and me, but I needed the confirmation all the same. "In and out," I said, reminding everyone, including myself. "We grab Cam, leave the flash drive in his cell with a note for Ms. Tremblay, then we get out of here. No detours, not even a trip to the bathroom, got it?"

The emergency lighting in the isolation unit was different than in the rest of the facility. The spotlight in each cube was positioned to shine directly down on whatever poor bastard was locked inside. And the lights had a blue tint to them, one that seemed brighter and more menacing than the lights upstairs.

The top step creaked under my weight, and I stopped in my tracks. On the off-chance Murphy was still posted down there, I didn't want to alert him to our presence.

Chris pushed past me, annoyed by my cautious approach. His tactic probably made more sense. Springing on the guard would give us the element of surprise, and hopefully give him less time to prepare.

I stared at the Taser in Chris's hand. Deadweight. Without another air cartridge, he couldn't reload it. Couldn't fire it. But he still clutched it in his hand like it had some value.

"Stay here," I said to Carly, then quickly made my way down the stairs after Chris. She didn't listen, but I wasn't surprised; it was her brother down there, after all.

"Guard," Chris called out, and I spun on my heels, half expecting to be tackled from behind. I caught a glimpse of Murphy behind the staircase, only his navy blue pants and black shoes visible. With no real weapon in sight, I grabbed a chair and lifted it over my head. The frame was metal and it was damn heavy; heavy enough to knock the guy out should he decide to make a move.

Chris took the left, and I took the right. Approaching Murphy from both sides meant he would at least be forced to choose between us. I was banking on that decision stalling out his brain for the half second I needed to hit him.

"Not moving," I said, suddenly noticing the angle of his shoes. His toes were pointed up toward the ceiling, which meant he was lying on his back and had a clear view of the staircase ... and us. Yet he hadn't so much as flinched when we made our approach.

"Shit," I hissed out as we slowly rounded the corner and looked down at him. He was dead, or at least he looked like he was.

Chris motioned for me to be ready, then eased in, his fingers spreading over the guard's neck. It wasn't until he shook his head, confirming what I already suspected, that I put the chair down.

Murphy's eyes were open and staring blankly up at the ceiling, a look of sheer agony clouding his expression. I despised that man, had vowed to make him pay for tasing me the way he did, but somehow, looking down into his vacant eyes, all that anger suddenly slipped away.

Chris rolled him over, looking for some sign of injury— a gash to the back of his head, a bullet wound, a protruding knife. But except for a purplish-blue bruise the size of a quarter on his temple, there was nothing.

"Keys are gone too," Chris said as he patted down the guard's pocket.

"Cam!" Carly's screech filled the isolation unit and I bolted upright, whacking my head on the underside of the stairs. My vision went spotty, and I reached out for something to grab onto. My foot snagged on the guard's pant leg, and I lost my balance. I fell to the floor and landed on top of Murphy, my eyes level with his, my fingers digging into the front of his shirt.

I tried to scramble up, but no matter what I did, no matter where I put my hands or where I braced my feet, I ended up tangled with him. I'd take a thousand live guards with their stun guns trained directly at my chest over this one dead one, who I couldn't seem to escape from, any day.

"I got you." Chris hauled me to my feet, his hands locking on my shoulders as he physically backed me away from the dead guard. "You're fine, man. Relax."

There was a dead man at my feet, a full-on riot erupting upstairs, and no lights to guide our way out. Apparently, Chris and I had very different ideas of what the word "fine" meant.

"Cam!" Carly screamed again, the deafening pitch of her voice refocusing my fear on her.

I flung my hands up, breaking Chris's hold on my shoulders, and made my way over to Carly. The doors to all three glass cells were open. She called out her brother's name a third time, and my mind finally processed what had her so panicked. Cam's cell, across from the one Chris and I had briefly occupied, was empty. The only clue that he'd ever been there was a neatly folded pile of clothes in the corner.

I walked in, bent down, and picked my way through the clothes in search of God knows what. Judging from the vile, nasty smell that wafted up each time I moved something, Cam had been wearing those clothes since the day they'd tossed him down here.

I picked up Cam's pants and shook them out, foolishly

hoping to find the guard's keys. Three white pills fell to the floor and rolled to a stop by Chris's feet. He reached down and grabbed them, turning them over in his hand before holding them out for me to see. I didn't recognize the three-letter marking etched into both sides, but I shoved them into my pocket anyway, thinking that when I got out of there, I'd look it up.

"Shit. Where the hell is he?" Chris asked, his eyes sweeping the area. "You remember him having anything in this cell when he was down here? Anything he could have used as a weapon?"

I dialed my memory back to the five hours we'd spent in that glass cage. I recalled Carly watching her brother, her shoulders curled in defeat as she tried unsuccessfully to get his attention. I remembered staring at the lights on the camera mounted on the ceiling, tapping out the seconds on my leg as I tried to figure out the pattern. And I clearly recalled Cam rocking back and forth in place, ignoring everything and everyone. But I didn't remember seeing a weapon, not even a piece of metal that could be whittled down into a shank. Even the toilet and bed in these glass cells were bolted to the floor.

"There's nothing down here he could've used," I finally said, coming to the same horrifying conclusion as Chris. Someone besides Murphy had been down here.

"We need to find him!" Carly was nearly hysterical, one panicked stream of demands after another falling from her lips. "There's got to be another way out of this area. I would've seen Cam come up. You would've seen him come up."

She was circling the isolation unit, running her hands

against the walls as if blindly searching for a secret exit. This wasn't part of the plan. Grab and go, that's all I'd signed up for when it came to Cam. A simple grab and go.

"We don't know where he is," I said as I pulled her away from the wall she was pounding on. It was solid cement, no chance of a hidden door anywhere in sight. "We don't even know if he's still alive or if he did this."

"You think Cam killed the guard?" Carly spun on me, her fists now meeting my chest. "You actually think Cam would hurt anybody?"

"Well, somebody killed the guard, and as far as I remember, the only one down here with him was your brother," Chris argued.

"Maybe you did it!" Carly raged.

Chris blew off that comment. "Like when? In my spare time? In between fighting my way out of that room and messing with the electrical panel? Or maybe when I had to feel my way back here because some mystery person smashed all the lights? Or maybe when I stumbled my way back to the lounge in search of Lucas because *you* said he was still trapped inside? Yeah, plenty of time for me to commit murder and stash that lunatic brother of yours somewhere safe."

Carly's eyes flashed wide at his words, her fists clenching at her sides. "Don't act like you weren't down here, because you were! You were in the basement, too, at the electrical panel. Who's to say you didn't do it?"

"For the record, the electrical panel isn't anywhere near the isolation cells. And besides, why the hell would I waste my time with a guard?" Chris was within two feet of her, forcing her backward into her brother's cell. "Or better yet," he continued, "if I killed him, why wouldn't I have simply dragged your brother with me when I was done?"

"How the hell should I know? You're the one with the faulty genes, not me."

"I swear to God, I'm so going to—"

Chris lunged for Carly. I blocked his path, my chest taking the full brunt of his rage, then shoved him into the cinderblock wall with enough force to let him know I wasn't joking around. "Both of you knock it off."

Chris shoved me off him. "She's the one that accused me of murder."

"You accused Cam first," Carly spit out. "Plus, you're the only one of us who's been alone."

I thought about challenging her on that, reminding her that I'd spent a fair amount of time searching for her by the door, only for her to tell me I was the one who was confused. But I doubted that would ease the quickly escalating situation. And besides, admitting that they were both technically unaccounted for when the guard was killed ... even I didn't even want to go there.

"You do anything besides mess with the electrical panel?" I asked Chris. His answer came out as an irritated "no," and I spun around to look at Carly. "Did you wait for me by the staircase like I told you to?" She nodded out a silent yes. "Then we're good."

THIRTY

I helped Carly search for an alternate exit while Chris took up residence in the guard's chair. He was pissed, and I didn't blame him. I had no right to question him, to even think for a second that he had anything to do with the guard's death. He was the only one in here I actually trusted. He had no obligation to Carly or me, yet he'd willingly signed on to this plan. The least I could do was show him some gratitude.

"What you said to Chris back there was wrong," I said to Carly as I checked behind the staircase for the third time. "Chris came back in here to help me, to help you. You'd do well to remember that."

Carly·ignored me, her hands trailing across the same cinderblock wall for the millionth time.

"You know, if Chris is messed up because some stupid genetic test says he is, then I am too. And so is your brother."

"That's not what I meant," she said, not even bothering to turn around. "I know you. I know Cam. But him," she said, "he's nobody to me."

"Well, I trust him, and he's the closest thing to a friend you have in here. So, from now on, I'd be careful what you say or you'll end up looking for Cam alone."

Carly went stone silent. Maybe it wasn't the nicest thing to say, but judging from the cold set of Chris's eyes, I'd say it was pretty damn accurate.

"Got it?" I asked, my thoughts scattering as I came across a door I'd never seen before. At first, it looked like a storage closet. Metal shelving covered the two side walls and the inside of the door was lined with hooks. But at the back end, there was another door partially hidden by a gazillion folded bedsheets neatly stacked on the floor.

"Found the sheets they took from our rooms," I said to Chris. I put my hand on the knob, paused, and looked back to make sure Chris had followed me. Regardless of what was on the other side of that door, I needed ... no, I wanted Chris at my back. He nodded, and I turned the handle, pushing the door wide to give us a clear view of whatever was lurking on the other side.

It took a second for my eyes to adjust to the darkness, but eventually I made out a staircase. Carly took off, the sound of her brother's name falling from her lips. She'd cleared the first few steps before either Chris or I had time to react, but I reached for her anyway, falling flat on my face as I tripped over a broom she'd knocked off the wall.

"You sure about this?" Chris asked, holding out a hand to help me up. "And I don't mean about the creepy staircase hidden behind a closet wall. I mean about *her*."

I sighed. No, I wasn't sure about Carly. Or the massive

shithole of promises I'd made to the kids upstairs. I wasn't sure about anything I'd done today, but it was a little too late to change my mind now.

Chris tipped his head toward the stairs. "She's a head case, Lucas. She can't control herself, and she's going to get you killed. I know they claim only one girl has ever tested positive for that gene, but if you ask me, she's got the same faulty wiring as her brother."

"She lost her sister, and you saw her brother." I understood how losing a sibling messed with your head. In a way, I could forgive her for being a little unpredictable.

"And you lost Tyler," Chris argued. "But you aren't crazy, and I'm *really* beginning to think that girl is."

I went to argue, to explain to him how lost and angry I was those first few weeks after Tyler's death, but Chris waved me off. "Listen," he said, his eyes darting toward the staircase Carly had just sprinted up. "I agreed to come in here because of you. Because you thought that somehow getting that information to Ms. Tremblay would shut this place down for good. And I did it because I know you're scared shitless that your sister will end up here. But I never agreed to chase Carly's ass all over this damn building. I will look for her this one time, but she does it again, and I'm out."

Nodding, I fixed my eyes on the narrow hallway at the top of the stairs. Chris wasn't wrong. He had no ties to Carly, and at the end of the day, my ties to her weren't strong enough to withstand much more of this either.

"Girl's more trouble than she's worth," Chris grumbled as he leapt over me and took the stairs two at a time.

We reached the top of the steps, and I scanned the hallway stretching out in front of us. "No way she made it far."

"She could be standing five feet from you and you wouldn't see her," Chris countered. "Without lights, this is a colossal waste of time."

A flashlight, a lantern, a damn match—I would've given my left arm for any one of those items right then. I couldn't see my own hand in front of my face, never mind figure out which way she'd gone.

I felt my way along the wall, my hand brushing up against what felt like a switch. Out of habit, I flicked it on. Nothing happened, and I slammed my hand into it. For all I knew, it wasn't even a light switch, rather some on-off button for the heating units.

"We can cover more ground if we split up," Chris suggested.

I shook my head, forgetting he couldn't see me, and said, "Absolutely not. I'm not searching for you once I find her."

"I vote for not finding her at all."

I was right there with him. I was literally "this close" to being able to sleep in my own bed, eat off a real plate, and argue with Suzie over the TV remote, and here I was, risking everything for a girl who'd pretty much called me a genetic freak.

"There," Chris said, pointing to a small hint of light at the end of the corridor.

I rushed toward it, trying to figure out where in the facility we were and how close the nearest exit door was. The light I was chasing spilled out from underneath a doorway and without thinking, I yanked it open. A series of emergency-lit corridors stretched out before me.

"You've got to be kidding me," Chris griped. "They only smashed that one light? Which means whoever did it knows our plan."

It all made sense now. The jammed lock, the glass by the door, the dark, disorienting corridors. Someone knew our plan and was systematically dismantling it piece by piece.

Chris caught me staring at his knuckles, and his eyes darkened with rage. "I already told you I. Didn't. Do it."

I knew that. It was actually the only thing I *did* know.

"You think someone heard us talking downstairs?" I asked, reaching for an explanation I already knew made no sense. The glass cells down there were soundproof, the intercoms couldn't function on generator power, and I'd made sure the red light on the security camera was off before I ever opened my mouth.

"Cam?" Chris suggested.

Even I knew that was a stretch. Cam would've had to have been pretty adept at lip reading, but to do even that, he would've had to pick his head up off his knees and actually acknowledge one of us. And as far as I knew, that never happened. "No. Not possible. Not the way he looked."

"You think—" Chris started to say, and I cut him off. I knew where his mind was going, and I didn't like it. Carly was emotional; I'd give him that. And trusting her to follow any sort of plan was dicey at best. But crazy enough to kill a guard and sabotage our whole plan? No way.

"You saw how scared Carly was when they dumped us

in the room with everybody else. Besides, we're her ticket out of here. Her *only* way out of here. Why would she sabotage a plan that solely benefits her?" I asked.

"Don't ask me," Chris replied. "She's your friend from the outside, not mine."

She wasn't my friend. She wasn't even Tyler's, but somehow guilt had made her my obligation. And lights or no lights, we were running out of time.

THIRTY-ONE

"We need help, somebody who knows the layout of this place," I said as I opened another door to an empty room. "There isn't time for us to search every room."

"You suggesting we ask Ms. Tremblay for help?"

I hated to admit it, but that's exactly what I was thinking. "We need to give her the flash drive anyway, so two birds, one stone, right?"

"And you're pretty confident that she isn't behind any of this? Because I'm not."

I shook my head. I trusted her about as much as I trusted the guards locked in that room, but I'd seen the way she watched Carly, remembered her plea that I keep Carly safe. The protectiveness I'd heard in her voice was genuine. If I could harness that, then maybe I could manipulate her into helping us.

"Great," Chris said, reluctantly agreeing with me. "Now I get to ask the one person I hate most in the world for help."

We searched for Carly as we went, ducking our heads

into countless empty rooms. The silence was unsettling, especially since we had no idea what we might find around each corner. Judging from the partitions around the toilets in some of the rooms, we'd found the girl's wing, the one that was in full operational order but never used. That, and there were actually sheets on the beds.

"This one's clear," I said, shutting the door behind me, then drawing a giant X on it. I'd heisted a black sharpie from a janitor's supply closet two corridors over and started marking the hallways and rooms we'd already searched. Twice already, it'd prevented us from re-entering an area we'd already walked through.

The wings were labeled—resident dorms, kitchen and maintenance, testing rooms. I paused, sighing in relief, when I came across the red plastic sign directing us toward the staff quarters. "This way," I said.

There were twelve rooms in this hall, six on each side. I took the left; Chris took the right. I knocked on the doors; he kicked them. I heard a noise coming from the last door he kicked, like a chair toppling over as someone scrambled to hide.

"Ms. Tremblay?" I shouldered my way in front of him and tried to make my voice sound as small and helpless as possible. "It's Lucas. Lucas Marshall. I need your help."

Chris went to kick the door again, and I put my hand up for him to stop. We needed Ms. Tremblay's help, and scaring the shit out of her wasn't the way to get it.

I tested the knob. It turned, and the door opened an inch before catching. Chain lock. Funny, with all the technology they had in this place, she still felt the need to use a centuries-old device.

"We can't find Carly," I said through the small gap in the door. "I was hoping she's with you."

A tiny sliver of her face came into view, her eyes narrowing on my hands. I held them up, palms out, to show her I was unarmed, then spun around and pulled my shirt out of my waistband so she could see I wasn't hiding a Taser. Her gaze shifted to Chris, and I motioned for him to do the same. "We aren't going to hurt you," I promised. "We really do need your help finding Carly. Is she with you?"

Ms. Tremblay closed the door, and I held my breath until I heard the clink of the chain coming loose. She opened the door fully and stepped out into the hall rather than letting us in.

"What do you mean, you can't find her?"

The edge of panic in her voice was a good sign. It meant she hadn't checked out entirely, that she might still care enough about what happened to Carly to help us.

"I got her out of that room like I promised. I was right behind her," I said, bending the truth. "But somebody pulled me back in, and by the time I fought my way back out, she was gone."

"What about the guards? Have you asked them for help?"

"No," I said. "They're still trying to get control of that room. You were there; you saw what it was like. I'm begging you, please help us find her."

She stood there silently for what seemed like an eternity, watching us, her head tilting from left to right as if trying to piece together a puzzle, debating whether to believe a word we were saying.

"We had an interesting conversation with an old friend of yours," Chris said. He'd given me a chance to try the pathetic and helpless route, and now he was going to do it his way. "One Joe Thompson. That name ring a bell to you?"

"How do you know Joe?" she asked.

We didn't, not really. But I didn't say that. That would require me telling her exactly who Carly was and why she was here, and I wasn't ready to do that. Not yet anyway.

"It doesn't matter how we know him. Let's just say we encountered him during our little adventure on the outside, and he was quite eager to get ahold of you," I said. "He even gave me a flash drive full of information he swore you'd be interested in, then pointed us back here."

She held out her hand, thinking I was simply going to hand the flash drive over.

"Not a chance," I said as I met her glare head-on. "You help us find Carly, and then *maybe* I'll consider handing it over."

She wavered for a minute, her eyes roaming over every inch of my body as if she was trying to figure out where I'd stashed it. I couldn't help it—I laughed. If she thought she had a chance in hell of parting me with that information before I was ready, then she was an idiot.

She sighed, seeming to accept our terms. "And how exactly is Carly involved in all this?" she asked.

"She's not," I quickly said.

She shook her head, no longer buying our story. "The

three of you are connected. Anybody who's spent more than five minutes with you could figure that out."

"Her name is Carly," I started, easing my way into the full truth with information she already knew. "Carly Denton."

"Denton?" The whispered name parted her lips, her mouth opening in a silent gasp as she made the connection.

"Cameron is her brother," I said, answering her unspoken question.

Ms. Tremblay swallowed hard, her eyes sliding from Chris to me. "And you know her how?"

"Lucas's brother, Tyler, used to date her sister," Chris replied. He seemed irritated, as if this little who's who game we were playing was nothing more than a waste of time, and he was trying to hurry it along by answering for me.

"Her name was Olivia," I said, filling in the rest. "She killed herself the day we buried Tyler. Cam is all Carly has left now."

"Sweet mother of God," Ms. Tremblay said as she backed up. "This isn't possible."

I nodded. "It is."

"But why is she here? Why in God's name would you drag a girl, a girl who has already been through so much, into a place like this?"

Technically, Carly had dragged *us* in here, but whatever. "She's here for her brother."

Ms. Tremblay stood there for a minute, a look of total confusion covering her face as she struggled to make sense of it all. The deaths. The gene. The madness that linked us all together.

"We have to find her," she finally said. "We need to get her out of here."

"Why the hell do you think we came looking for you?" Chris asked. "You got a map of this place? Like a floor plan or something? We can't find her if we don't know where the hell we are."

She started walking down the hall, gesturing for us to follow. "I don't need a map. I know where every door leads. The guard in the basement—Murphy—he made sure I had the layout memorized in case something like this happened. He can—"

"He's dead," Chris blurted out.

Ms. Tremblay stumbled into the wall, her face going impossibility white. "*Dead.*" She mouthed that one word over and over, never once speaking it out loud as she paced the hall, fighting off tears she obviously didn't want us to see.

"How is that possible?" It didn't take a genius to figure out that she and Murphy were more than simply colleagues.

"No clue. We found him sprawled out in the isolation unit," Chis said, unfazed by her distress. "My money is on Cam, though."

"Cam?" she mumbled in disbelief. "Impossible. Murphy was armed and outweighed him by at least fifty pounds. And Cam … he was … "

"Was what?" Chris took a step closer, towering over Ms. Tremblay. "Not all there? Mentally toast? A walking veg—"

"Sedated," Ms. Tremblay corrected. "He's on an eight-hour regimen. Murphy knows that. All the guards here know that. He would've given him a dose shortly after we'd pulled you two up into the staff lounge."

I thought back to the three white pills I'd found in Cam's glass cell, the ones I'd shoved in my pocket for some unknown reason. I pulled them out and dropped them into her hand. "I think it's safe to say he hasn't taken one in a while."

"Where's Cam now?" she asked, closing her fist around the pills.

"Beats me," Chris said. "His cell is empty."

"Empty!" she gasped. "We need to find him. We need to find them both."

THIRTY-TWO

We filled Ms. Tremblay in on the smashed emergency lights as we walked, opting to leave out the part about Chris screwing with the electrical panel. More than once, she asked about seeking help from the other guards, and each time we came up with an excuse, hurrying her in the opposite direction under the false claim that we'd "thought" we'd seen Carly. I knew we'd have to go back to that room eventually, see with our own eyes what we'd manipulated those boys into doing. But if I had my way, I'd avoid it as long as possible.

"Even if Cam wasn't sedated, if somehow he managed to spit his pills out, I don't think he would've hurt Murphy," Ms. Tremblay said. She'd been talking through scenarios for the past ten minutes, each one always ending up the same way. Uncertain.

"What makes you say that?" Up till then, I'd held back from asking her, afraid she'd insist on seeing Murphy for herself, further stalling our search. But I was pissed and more than a little bit curious as to why she insisted on defending

Cam, the only guy in the Bake Shop who'd actually shown violent tendencies.

"I've been thinking about it, and it just doesn't make sense," she said, searching the kitchen for any sign of Carly or her brother. "Cam wasn't violent, not the way everybody thought."

I didn't agree, given that he'd apparently knocked his roommate out and then hung him with his own bedsheets, but whatever. Arguing with her right now wasn't going to get us anywhere.

"He showed distinct signs of distress his first night here," Ms. Tremblay continued, "but nothing I would categorize as unusual. And he's never lashed out at any of the guards or me. He was more withdrawn than anything. The first time I spoke with him, he begged to be sent home. He wasn't aggressive or even angry like the rest of you. He was petrified, so much so that I placed him on suicide watch."

"What did you expect?" Chris asked. "You ship us up here, treat us like a bunch of lab rats, and you expect us to be cheery and cooperative?"

"No. I suppose not," she mumbled, but even that little concession wasn't particularly gratifying. It couldn't erase the four weeks of testing I'd suffered through, and it definitely couldn't bring Tyler back.

"By the second day of testing, Cam had completely shut down, refused to respond to any form of stimulus. I told the guards to ease up, but they insisted that he was just being defiant. They called the supervising office in Washington and had them send up orders to step up the protocol, push Cam harder."

"And ... " Chris prompted.

"I talked to Murphy. He convinced the medic to at least do another physical exam, look for self-inflicted wounds—something I could use to get them to stop testing him for a little bit," Ms. Tremblay continued. "Cam thrashed around the entire time, and Murphy had to strap him to the exam table in order for the medic to do something as simple as check his heart rate. And even then, Cam kept begging us to let him go before he ended up dead."

"Are you saying he tried to kill himself?" I asked, desperately trying to shut out images of Tyler sitting in the lawn chair in our backyard, the empty bottle of pills on the ground next to a fifth of whiskey.

"No," she replied. "Cam was covered in defensive wounds. His chest and back were bruised beyond belief."

"They beat him?" I ground out, remembering the look in Ryan's eyes, the way he'd singled out that one guard he wanted dead. Is that what they'd done to Cam ... beat him into submission?

"No, not any of the guards," Ms. Tremblay clarified. "I made sure of that. It took days for Murphy to get me the footage from the surveillance camera in Cam's bunk room. And even then, he had to make up some story to the guards about wanting some time alone with me in the control room."

"Okay," I said. "So, who did it then?"

"When the guards were instructed to intensify Cam's testing, they took upon themselves to back off when his roommate got physical. They thought that extra note of aggression would be the perfect stressor. Cam may have killed his roommate, but I don't believe he did it because of his genetic profile. He was afraid, and he had good reason to be from what I saw. He did it because he had no choice."

"And the guards who stood by and watched all this, the doctor who was overseeing the testing—what happened to them?"

"They were dismissed," she said. "That's why we moved your group out in spite of the storm. We were understaffed. And that's why we moved everyone into the lounge earlier. There wasn't enough staff to monitor your individual rooms once the generators failed."

"So the plan was to keep Cam down there, drugged up, forever?" Chris asked.

"No. I was only trying to keep him comfortable until I could have him transferred to an inpatient facility," Ms. Tremblay explained. "Cam wasn't down there as some sort of punishment; he was on suicide watch. I was overseeing his care myself. I was in the process of making arrangements for him to be admitted to an adolescent psychiatric facility closer to his home. I thought being nearer to family might help."

I thought about challenging that, informing her that Cam had been within ten feet of his sister for over five hours and he hadn't so much as flinched. There wasn't a person alive—friend or family—who could help Cam now.

Chris cursed long and hard. "Did Cam's family know this? Did his sister or his parents have any clue that you weren't planning on locking him up for good?"

I'd been wondering the same thing but was too afraid to ask. If we'd left well enough alone, Cam might be home or near his family, Chris and I would be bitching our way through the reintegration phase, and there wouldn't be twelve kids, with their drivers and guards, lying dead at the bottom of some ravine.

"Yes, Cam's family knew about the incident and that he was being held longer than the rest of his group," she replied. "But no, they didn't know about his possible transfer. His treatment plan hadn't been finalized yet, and I didn't want to give them false hope."

False hope was better than nothing. Those kids lying dead at the bottom of that ravine would've taken false hope over the fate the Bake Shop had handed them any day.

THIRTY-THREE

We continued to search for Cam and Carly in silence, checking every nook and cranny of the Bake Shop's large industrial kitchen. No matter how hard I tried to push the thought aside, my mind kept circling back to the idea that Ms. Tremblay knew what this place was doing to us. She'd witnessed it with Tyler and Cam, and yet she'd done nothing but sit back and let them continue poking at us.

"Why?" I asked. "Can you tell me why, after knowing what happened to Cam, you did nothing to help any of us?"

She sighed, her eyes looking everywhere but at me. "Sometimes the ends justify the means, Lucas. If we could only find a way to identify those with a proven potential to become violent offenders, do you know how much safer the world would be?"

I'd heard all that crap before. Some government-paid scientist had discovered an anomaly while studying the brain of a school shooter, a "kink in the warrior gene," he'd first called it. A couple of trips to Congress and a promise to end the youth-violence epidemic that seemed to dominate the nightly news, and bam, our government wrote him a billion-dollar check to develop a dozen facilities just like the one we were trapped in.

I slammed a pantry door with more force than necessary and twisted around to face her. "Do you have any idea what your stupid testing does to us?" I yelled. "Do you even care? I've done nothing wrong. Chris did nothing wrong. Tyler did nothing wrong. Yet here we are, your own personal science experiment, because some scientist who probably doesn't even have kids of his own decided screwing with our minds was a good idea."

Ms. Tremblay shook her head. "Your brother wasn't adjusting well, Lucas. We shouldn't have let him go. *I* shouldn't have let him go."

"That's where you're wrong. You shouldn't have brought him here to begin with," I said, hoping that she'd let go of her save-the-world philosophy and admit it. Just once, admit that what they were doing here was wrong.

"I had a child once," she said, and I tossed my hand out in a *so what* gesture. Joe had pretty much said that was the reason she'd changed sides, that her husband and daughter's deaths somehow convinced her that these facilities were the key to her revenge. I didn't much care.

"Her name was Emily," she whispered, her eyes glossing with the memory. "We were travelling through Philadelphia. Sam—her dad—and I were at a conference in Atlanta, a preliminary hearing about IGT's claim that they'd found a correlation between the MAOA-L gene and the propensity to commit violent crimes. Emily's nanny was sick with the flu, so we'd brought her along with us."

"Good for you," I said, irritated that she'd stopped looking for Carly altogether and was now standing in the middle of the kitchen, reminiscing.

"Let me guess—your husband was a geneticist of some sort?" Chris snapped.

"No," she said, "he was a psychologist like me. A profiler."

I laughed at the irony of it all, wondering what he'd make of us.

"We were on our way home. I was driving; Sam was on the phone with Joe. Both of them were opposed to what IGT was proposing."

According to Joe, so were you, I silently added.

"I pulled off the highway, not even thinking about where I was. We needed gas, and Emily had been complaining about having to go to the bathroom for the past hour. We should've gotten back on the highway as soon as I saw the neighborhood, but the gas light was on, and, well ... " Ms. Tremblay trailed off. She didn't need to fill in the blanks; I knew what had happened next.

"I waited in the car while Sam brought her in to use the bathroom. They were victims of circumstance, 'wrong place, wrong time,' or so the police told me. They caught the person who did it, but he died awaiting trial, some gang-related incident in prison." She paused and looked at me. I don't know what she expected to see. Understanding? Forgiveness, perhaps.

"If we'd known about the gene, if we could've identified

his potential to become violent, then we could've removed him from society."

"Then what?" Chris prompted. "Your husband and daughter would still be alive?"

"Yes," Ms. Tremblay whispered. "I lost everything that day. Everything. Over something that should've been preventable. *Is* preventable."

"And you're assuming the guy who killed your family was defective? That he carried that same gene as me and Lucas?" Chris asked, and she nodded her answer.

"The files," Chris said, nudging my arm. "Give her the damn flash drive."

It was time. I bent down and yanked off my sneaker and sock. "Here," I said as I placed the flash drive in her hand. "That guy who shot your family, they *did* test him." Or so Joe had told me. "And he wasn't a carrier. He was just some random guy, doped up on heroine."

I closed her fingers around the flash drive, squeezing a little harder than necessary. "It's all on there. You should think about that next time you lock one of us up in your little lab and play with our minds."

Ms. Tremblay whirled around and walked out of the kitchen, muttering something incoherent under her breath. Chris shot me a *what do you want to do* look, and I shrugged before following her out.

She ducked into a room to the left, leaving the door open for me and Chris. There was a massive TV on the far wall, and it wasn't until I was within touching distance of the screen that I realized it was actually twenty-four frameless monitors all hung side by side. A U-shaped table was positioned in the center of the room, keyboards and laptops littering the surface. And in the corner, spilling out of a cardboard box, were what looked like broken surveillance cameras.

Ms. Tremblay went down the row of laptops, hitting the power button on each one. The fifth one down lit up, the tiny blue light flickering to life. She inserted the flash drive and waited impatiently, her fingers drumming the enter key until the information she was searching for finally scrolled across the screen. She scanned the documents so fast, I doubted she'd even begun to appreciate the extent of Joe's research. But apparently the small glimpse she got was more than enough.

She yanked the flash drive from the laptop and shoved it into her pocket. "Does anybody besides the two of you know about this?"

"No," I lied. Sob story about her daughter or not, I still wasn't a hundred percent sure I trusted her.

"Good," she said. "For now, keep it that way."

THIRTY-FOUR

"You gave Ms. Tremblay the information, so I say we cut bait and get out of here now," Chris said.

"What about Cam? What about Carly?" I asked, looking behind us. Ms. Tremblay had told us to go ahead, that she'd catch up with us shortly. Something about making sure none of the documents she'd downloaded had made their way to the facility's mainframe. But that was at least five minutes ago, and we hadn't seen her since.

"Screw them," Chris replied. "Carly's been nothing but trouble since the second we laid eyes on her, and you saw Cam. He's pretty much checked out already."

I shook my head. "You can go if you want, but I can't just leave Carly in here. Not after what Ms. Tremblay said about the guards and her brother. He—"

I stopped mid-sentence, the hint of a shadow at the end of the hall catching my attention. I turned around, half expecting it to be one of the guards from the lounge or Cam. But the shadow was already gone. "Did you see that?"

"See what?" Chris asked. He walked down the entire length of the hall, then turned back and tossed his hands out, silently asking what had me so spooked.

"Nothing," I said, shaking off the feeling that I was being watched. "I swear this place is screwing with me even more than usual."

"You and me both," Chris said as he pulled up next to me. "There's nobody down there. But the fact that you're starting to see things makes me think I'm right. We need to get the hell out of here before you crack next."

"Can't," I said. As infuriating as Carly was, I couldn't leave her.

Rounding the corner, I stopped dead in my tracks. It was another empty hall, but something about this one felt familiar. Agonizingly familiar. The white tiles that lined the floor, the graying grout, the small red streak on the wall that I'd always assumed was blood they couldn't get off...

"Our room," Chris said, and we both ducked in. The beds were stripped bare, the uncomfortable squares of foam they called pillows waiting for the new residents. Ones who'd never made it here. Ones who were lying dead in a van. The camera mounted in the corner of our room was off, its giant eye hanging downward like a wayward child. I motioned for Chris to give me a lift, then reached up and tore it off the ceiling. I threw it to the floor, driving my foot into the lens until it was nothing more than a broken mess of wires. It felt amazing to actually destroy some little piece of this place.

"How could we have left this behind?" Chris laughed,

and I turned around, found him lounging on the top bunk, the magazine I'd stashed in my mattress open in his hands.

"If you're done reminiscing?" Ms. Tremblay was standing in the doorway, her hands waving at us to get moving. She saw the magazine and sighed in disgust, but made no move to take it away. I guess in the scheme of things, one dirty magazine didn't matter much anymore.

Chris tucked the magazine back into the slit I'd cut in the mattress—a present for the next unlucky soul who got stuck in this room—then jumped down off the top bunk.

I headed toward the door, paying more attention to Chris kicking at the shattered surveillance camera than to where I was going, and I walked smack into Ms. Tremblay's back. I smothered a curse, wondering why the person who'd been bitching at us to hurry up a few seconds earlier was now stopped dead in her tracks. There were nine rooms in this hall, nine empty rooms that all needed to be searched.

There was a shuffling sound just behind Cam's doorway; nothing but an echo of movement. I walked in, half expecting Cam to be sitting there, rocking back and forth, completely oblivious to the fact that we were all searching for him. He wasn't, but finding him in that broken state would've been a blessing compared to what I actually saw.

Carly.

Her tiny frame was huddled into the corner of her brother's room. Her eyes were red and she was trembling, her words slurring together into what sounded like the phrase "too late." It wasn't until I passed through the doorway that I saw him hanging there. The bedsheet was wrapped around the metal frame of the top bunk, and Cam's legs were dangling inches off the ground. He'd wound the sheet twice around the frame, ensuring it would hold, before slipping off the opposite end and snapping his neck.

"Oh shit." I wrapped my hands around Cam's legs and lifted him up, pointlessly trying to ease the tension of the noose. "Help me get him down."

Chris scrambled up to the top bunk and clawed at the sheet until it tore free. Cam fell forward, his entire weight slumping over my shoulder. Unable to stop our momentum, I tumbled to the ground, Cam's lifeless body landing on top of me.

"Move," Chris yelled, and I slid Cam to the floor, then skidded backward out of the way.

Chris knelt down next to Cam and pressed an ear to his mouth, listening for signs that Cam was still breathing. He rotated his wrist to feel for a pulse, then swore and started alternating between pounding on Cam's chest and forcing his own breath into his lungs. Cam's chest rose and fell in time with Chris's breathing, but not once did he gasp for air. Not once did he look anything but gone.

For a few excruciatingly long minutes, my entire life revolved around Chris's hands on Cam's chest, Carly's ragged whimpers behind me, and the agonizing sense of despair gripping us all. Chris's hands slowed to a stop as he lifted two trembling fingers to Cam's neck. He shook his head and fell backward, his entire body collapsing onto the cold tile floor as he covered his face with his hands.

I knew what Chris was thinking: we'd failed. We'd risked

everything to come in here, had put ten other boys' lives in danger, and for what? None of it had changed a damn thing.

"No," I screamed as I shoved Chris out of the way and started pounding on Cam's chest myself. "I didn't risk everything, *everything*, for it to end this way."

"Stop." Ms. Tremblay laid her hand on my shoulder, gently squeezing until she had my attention. "He's gone, Lucas. He's gone."

I leaned back, staring down at Cam's dead eyes. They were a darker blue than Carly's and filled with a pain that went soul-deep. I knew that look; I'd seen Tyler surrender to it in our backyard.

Bloody handprints marred Cam's bare chest, the deep crimson standing out against his pale skin. I tilted his head to the side, looking for claw marks, scratches, something to indicate that he'd fought—that the second the sheet had tightened around his neck, he'd changed his mind and struggled to live. But as with Tyler, I found nothing. Not a single outward sign that he'd had any second thoughts. Any desire to live.

I slid the makeshift noose off Cam's neck, flinching at the deep purple ring that ran from his jaw to the back of his ears. I screamed as memories flooded my mind. One after another they bombarded me, like flashes from that strobe light above my bed, burning my eyes and searing my very being. The rage built to a strangling level, and I stood up and slammed my fist into the wall.

"He killed himself," I muttered numbly. "He went through all of this, for what? What's the point of getting out of this place, of going home at all, if this is what will happen? If eventually we'll just give up?"

"No," Chris said. "We're not them. You're not Tyler and I'm not Cam. This won't happen to us. I won't let it."

I laughed, the harsh sound hurting even my own ears. "First my brother, then Olivia, and now Cam? Odds aren't exactly in our favor."

"We're *not* them," Chris repeated, and I wondered who he was trying to convince—me or himself.

I wished I had half his faith, but everything I'd seen, everything I'd lived through, demanded that I believe otherwise. I dug the heel of my hands into my eyes, refusing to cry, refusing to give this place even an ounce of my pain.

"Lucas?" Ms. Tremblay laid a hand on my shoulder, her tone soft and pitiful. For a second I was back home again, loosening my tie after Tyler's funeral, listening to the minister try and comfort my mother by saying some stupid shit about how Tyler was at peace.

"You won," I said, flinching her off. "Are you happy now?"

"No." Her voice hitched, and I looked up and saw tears pooling in her eyes. Genuine tears. "It's going to be all right," she said. "Somehow, I'm going to make this all right."

"How?" I stood up and looked in Carly's direction. She was crumpled on the floor, sobbing uncontrollably. She reminded me so much of the Cam I'd seen in the isolation unit earlier, lost in a world of agony with no desire to come back. "How are you going to make any of this better?" I asked.

"I'm going to get you home. I'm going to get you all home."

"Home." I tossed that ugly word in her direction, knowing full well that whatever life I'd had died the second that stupid genetic test declared me a potential killer. Suzie and my mom were it, the only ones who didn't look at me with a mixture of disgust and fear. No girlfriend. No college acceptance letters. No future to speak of. Absolutely nothing to look forward to. Nothing to live for.

THIRTY-FIVE

Chris was kneeling in front of Carly, running his hand along the side of her face as he tried to ease her pain. She all but ignored him, sat there with her hands locked around her knees, refusing to answer any of his questions.

"Carly?" I knelt down beside Chris and ducked my head to meet her eyes. I needed Carly to know that I was going to keep my word, that I'd been where she was and somehow, someway, I'd get her through this. "I'm going to take you home now. Nick and Joe are waiting outside."

"I won't leave without Cam," she said as she crawled over to her brother, picked up his head, and laid it in her lap. "You promised me we'd bring him home."

The sadness in her tone splintered me, adding another layer of unbearable weight to my already sinking shoulders. Cam wasn't the only one who deserved a chance to go home. There were ten boys in that room—five who I'd promised freedom to—and I'd left them in there to die. My mind flickered to Ryan and his reluctance to tell me his name, his hesitancy to trust anybody. I'd harnessed his fear and used it against him with barely a second thought.

"We won't leave him here, Carly. We won't leave any of them here," I promised.

"Lucas," Chris whispered. I followed his eyes to the corner of the room, to the cramped space I'd first found Carly huddled in. Lying there on the ground was what looked like a bat. Or the wooden leg to a table. I'd have to pick it up to be sure, but it was caked in dried blood. And if I wasn't mistaken, that was hair.

Ms. Tremblay saw it too. "This is my fault," she muttered to herself. "If I'd just taken Joe's calls. If I'd called the Dentons myself. This is all my fault."

I nodded, not even considering easing her guilt. It *was* her fault, her's and every government official's who developed these facilities. "There's nothing left in here for Carly," I told her. "I need to get her home. *You* need help me get her home."

Ms. Tremblay nodded and reached out to Carly, whispering soft words of encouragement as she helped her off the ground. "You need keys to unlock the front door," she said.

I held out my hand. Ms. Tremblay had keys; I'd watched her use them to let us in.

"I don't have them. I left everything—my keys, my staff ID, everything—in my room."

"Who else has keys?" I asked, cringing as I anticipated her answer.

"All the guards have a full set. There's a master key. It's the only one with a code sequence that starts with a number nine.

It opens every room in this building, including the outside gates."

———————

It took some convincing, but I finally managed to get Carly to move. She was shuffling along beside me, her hand locked in mine. Ms. Tremblay had wandered off, muttering something about the master key. I doubted she'd find it. She seemed quite sure that she'd left everything useful back in that room, more concerned about getting herself out than taking her purse and keys. I'd let her look anyway. Something in her eyes had told me she needed to keep moving, to try and do something useful to keep her mind off the horror unfolding around her.

It was surprisingly easy to find our way back to the staff lounge, like some sick, magnetic pull had us turning in the right direction. Every. Single. Time. The faint glow of that lone emergency light came into view, a beacon daring us step closer.

"We should get some more flashlights if we can," Chris said, the narrow beam of his light skirting across the floor. "Who the hell even knows what time it is anymore, and I don't want to spend my night trudging through the snow in the complete darkness." We only had one flashlight between the three of us, and it barely worked. We'd found it stuffed inside a moldy crate in the back of a utility closet with a bunch of other half-broken items.

"And we're going to need something to dig out the glass in the lock." I said, cursing myself for not grabbing that blood-coated club we'd found in Cam's old bunk room.

Maybe I could've use it to pry the glass loose, or at the very least shatter it free.

The sound of crushed glass beneath my shoes had me reaching back, swiping the flashlight from Chris's hand. The light above the door had been smashed, and the chunk of glass I remembered seeing wedged into the lock was gone.

Chris started moving, his shadow creeping away from my line of sight. "Wait," I called out, training the flashlight at the floor. He looked down, his eyes narrowing as he traced the outline of the shoeprint with the toe of his sneaker.

"No blood," I whispered to Chris, remembering that the kids in that room had been stripped of their shoes and socks, the sharp glass just waiting to meet their bare feet.

Chris eased the door open, both of us waiting for the echo of feet, the flare of a Taser gun, something to come at us. Wanting to draw someone out, I kicked a pile of glass into the room, hoping they'd mistake it for me. All I got in return was silence.

With more courage than was probably wise, I ducked my head inside, shining the flashlight from side to side, my eyes skirting over the bodies sprawled across the room. They were huddled close together, making it nearly impossible to distinguish one body from the next in the dark.

A boot came into view and I dropped to the ground, making myself as small a target as possible. I crawled into the room and ran my hand up the guard's legs, feeling around his utility belt for a flashlight. Keys were no longer my first priority; I needed to flood this room with light so I could see what had happened.

I found a flashlight tucked behind the extra air cartridges for the Taser gun the guard still had clutched in his hand. I tossed it to Chris, motioning for him to keep it turned off. I wanted each of us armed with a gun and a flashlight before we made our move.

"Utility belts," I whispered to Chris. He dropped to the ground and made his way around the opposite side of the room, searching each body as he went.

In a matter of minutes, Chris and I had five flashlights, three stun guns, and a rather impressive-looking knife in our possession. But no keys. I patted down every single body I came across—guard and resident alike—but found nothing. Not one lone key.

On Chris's cue, we hit our flashlights at the same time, and light illuminated the room.

"Holy crap." I wasn't sure if it was Chris or I who said that, but it didn't matter. It aptly described what we saw.

The five guards and the medic were all still there, each one face-down, blood pouring from every opening in their bodies. They'd been bludgeoned with something, something large enough to do some serious damage. I swept my flashlight across the floor and saw it—a weapon similar to the one I'd seen back in Cam's bunk room. Someone had dismantled the only table in the room—the bolts where they'd pried it from the ground were still sticking out—and used the legs as clubs.

"Ryan," I called out, praying he'd respond. Needing him to respond. I'd targeted him, seen the broken look in his eyes and used him anyway. Of everybody in here, it was his eyes that would haunt my dreams and leave me begging for a forgiveness I didn't deserve.

"Can we go now?"

I whipped the flashlight in the direction of Ryan's voice. On either side of him were the twins, both alive. Bruised and bloody, but alive.

I took a tiny step in Ryan's direction and he shrank back, melding himself with the wall. He looked terrified of me, and I hadn't even touched him. Slowly, I squatted down and ducked my head to meet his eyes, hoping he'd see that I meant him no harm. "What happened?"

His gaze skirted to Carly and I snapped my fingers in front of him, refocusing his attention on me. I was afraid of this, afraid that once they let a tiny piece of the anger out, they wouldn't be able to pull it back in. And Carly was an easy target. The girl who wasn't even supposed to be here. The girl who'd set everything in motion.

I stood up and tucked her behind my body. "You look at me, not her," I said. "She's with me, got it? Now, tell me what happened."

My response was met with another repetitive request from Ryan, this one more forceful. "Can. We. Go. Now?"

I thought about questioning him, but something about the way he was huddled there, his back against the wall, sandwiched between the only two other kids alive in that room, told me he'd all but given up.

Chris shone his flashlight at the door before swinging it back toward one of the dead guard's feet. "The floor in the hallway is covered with glass, so you may want to take their boots."

I stopped Ryan as he went to pass by me. I'd promised him his freedom, and after everything I'd put him through, I sure as hell was going to deliver. "Wait for us by the front door. There are people outside, friends of mine, who'll help us."

THIRTY-SIX

We did what we could—closed their eyes and tried our best not to disturb them—but in the end, the sight of all those kids lying there, four boys still attached to the probe end of a stun gun, did me in. There was no panic here, no sense of urgency to save myself like I'd felt in the van. I had time, as much time as I needed, to check for pulses, but I couldn't bring myself to do it, couldn't face the fact that in my attempt to cause a mere distraction, I'd killed them all.

I'd barely made it to the hall before I heaved up the contents of my empty stomach, the caustic bile no match for my guilt.

Chris was still in the room, methodically checking each body, while I stayed in the hall, slumped against the wall, too much of a wuss to even face what I'd done.

"All dead," Chris said, inducing another wave of nausea from me. "If it makes you feel better, I think the guards did most of the damage."

It didn't. Plus, it still made me puzzled about who killed Murphy.

"Do you think Cam did this?" Chris asked as he handed me a rag. I looked at the white cloth, wondering which dead body he'd lifted it off of. My eyes settled on the jagged edge of his T-shirt, and I realized what he'd done—ripped a piece off his own shirt and given it to me. For the second time that day.

"Who else could have done it?" I whispered, not wanting Carly to hear. She was still standing inside the door; she hadn't moved from that spot since the first beam of her flashlight lit up the room. I think it was shock, or maybe fear, that had her immobilized. Either way, the look on her face as she took in the room was bad. "You saw the table leg in Cam's room. It was covered with blood."

"Yeah, that's what I was thinking, but there's no blood on the floor out here," Chris said, swinging his light across the glass-ridden tile, then down the hall. "I don't remember seeing shoes on Cam, not to mention he'd left all his clothes behind. Anybody walking out of here in bare feet would have left one hell of a trail."

"Maybe he grabbed shoes from somewhere else?" I proposed, grasping for explanations I knew were absurd.

"I doubt it. There are only three sets of shoes missing off the guards, and Ryan and the twins just took them."

"I don't know. No way was it Ms. Tremblay," I said, remembering her reaction when I'd told her about Murphy dead in the isolation unit. Plus, she didn't strike me as the overly violent type; more of a psychological tormentor. As much as I never thought I'd believe it, she wasn't that different from us. She hadn't wanted anyone to die, was actually trying to save people. But like with everything Chris and I had done so far, she'd failed. Turned all of her intentions into some warped version of a singular good thought.

"All six of the guards in this facility are accounted for," Chris said. "Five dead up here, one dead downstairs. The medic too."

"Please tell me you have some idea of where to go from here?" I begged. I was spent, my mind incapable of forming a coherent thought, never mind a back-up plan.

"What do you mean, 'where to go from here'?" Chris asked. "You gave Ms. Tremblay Joe's files. We found Carly, and Cam is dead. We're done. Nothing else to do but leave."

I nodded, one hundred percent on board with that plan.

"Carly?" I reached for her shoulder, gently guiding her out of the room.

"I just want to go home," she said, tears clouding her eyes. "I want to go back home and forget any of this ever happened."

The pain I heard in her voice ripped me in two. She'd never be able to unsee Cam hanging from the end of that bedsheet. Shit, I still saw Tyler's empty stare every time I closed my eyes. Every time I walked by the music store he used to work at on the weekends. Every time I looked at my mom or Suzie. Carly could beg, plead, drink herself into a stupor, but that image would never go away.

"I'm going to take you home. I promise," I said. "But I need to go back in the lounge for a second and look for keys to the front gates. I need you to stay here, right here, while Chris and I do that, okay?"

Without a word, Carly reached into the pocket of her sweatshirt, pulled out a set of keys, and dropped them into my hand. Digging her hand back into her pocket, she pulled out another set, then another, until all six sets lay in the palm of my hand.

"Where did you get these?" I asked.

"From them," she said. "From the guards in there and the one in the basement."

I shook my head, trying to wrap my brain around what she was saying. I'd been the first one into the lounge, had crawled across the floor checking the guards one at a time. But Carly hadn't moved an inch until I'd dragged her out. How did she end up with all their keys?

I looked at Chris, hoping he knew something I didn't. Maybe Carly had helped him search the guards while I was puking. Maybe he'd found the keys and tossed them to her as he continued checking the bodies. Maybe Ryan had handed them to her on his way out.

Maybe I was losing my mind.

"If you had these keys this entire time, then why the hell did you let Ms. Tremblay go off looking for them? Why did you let Lucas and I paw through the guards' pockets?"

"Because Ms. Tremblay's not one of us. She doesn't get to come out of here alive."

"What?" I dropped the keys I was holding to the floor and wheeled around to face her. "What the hell are you talking about?"

"I know who she is, and I know what she did to Cam. She's the one that had him thrown in that isolation cell to begin with, would've gladly left him locked up there forever. Cam deserved a second chance. She doesn't."

"Did Cam do this?" I asked, flicking my hand toward the lounge door. God knew how long she'd been sitting in the bunk room with her brother; she could have easily seen the keys in his room and taken them.

"No," she replied, setting off a new round of sobs. "He's dead."

I took a deep breath, reminding myself to be patient. "I know he's dead, Carly, but do you think he was capable of killing the guards?"

"No, Cam didn't kill anybody. Why does everybody keeping thinking he did?"

"Maybe because he already has," Chris muttered, drawing a warning glare from me.

"You don't know him at all. You think you do, but you don't. Nobody does."

"I know you're scared, Carly, and I get that you're just trying to protect your brother, but I need to know. Did Cam have these keys? Did you find them in his room?"

"It wasn't him," she replied. "He doesn't want to hurt anybody. He just wants to be left alone."

Her response had me wondering exactly how close she'd come to Cam in those last few hours, how she could possibly know what Cam had wanted. "How do you know this?"

"Because he smiled when he saw me. For a second I thought he knew who I was. That he was actually happy to see me," Carly said. "But I don't think he was happy at all," she continued. "I don't even think he really saw me. He was just…I don't know, happy to be free."

Free? "Wait. What? When did you talk to Cam?" Other

than finding him hanging from the bedframe, the only time Carly and Cam had been within eyesight of each other was in the isolation unit, and then they'd had six inches of sound-proof glass between them. "When did you talk to Cam?"

"In his room, right before he killed himself."

THIRTY-SEVEN

Not once had I ever seen Chris speechless. He was always the one with a quick joke aimed at calming me down and keeping me sane. But there he was, standing in the middle of the dark corridor, staring at this twig of a girl with absolutely nothing to say.

At least his mouth was closed; mine kept dropping open, no words, not a single sound ever coming out.

"I found him standing outside his room, staring at the bunk bed, talking to somebody. At first I thought it was you and Chris, but the room was empty. There was nobody there."

I closed my eyes and willed the memories away. Tyler had done the same thing; he would slip into dark trances, muttering unthinkable things, then cock his head as if listening to a reply that no one but him could hear.

"I reached for Cam's hand. I thought I could pull him back from wherever he was, but he lost it on me, pushed me aside and started screaming. He accused me of things I never did, called me names I didn't recognize. They let him beat him, did you know that? His roommate—they let his roommate beat him, on purpose. The guards actually placed bets on how soon he'd snap."

I shook my head, swallowing back my anger. Ms. Tremblay hadn't mentioned that the guards placed wagers on it.

"He laughed," Carly continued. "It was this twisted sound of hatred. And then he turned on me. He wrapped his hands around my neck and swore he'd kill me."

I stepped forward, my hand going to the zipper of her sweatshirt. Yanking it down, I pushed the fabric aside. Her neck was bruised, deep purple welts marring her skin.

"What else did he do?" I asked. The words rumbled from my chest, my anger riding so close to the surface that I wondered if I'd finally snap. If I'd survived all their tests only to lose it now.

"I started crying, rattling off every single memory I could think of, hoping he'd realize who I was and let me go. Nothing seemed to work, and his grip just tightened until I mentioned Olivia and Tyler."

"What about Tyler?"

"I reminded him of what happened to your brother, how Tyler had given in to them, let this place win. Cam was better than that, stronger than that, and I told him so."

I stepped back, my body meeting the hard, unforgiving wall behind me. Tyler wasn't weak; he was the strongest person I knew. "They broke him. This place broke him."

"He let me go then," Carly continued, ignoring my ramblings. "He mumbled an apology and sank down in the corner. You should've seen him. I couldn't get him to move, couldn't even get him to lift his head off of his knees. He was gone, completely gone. I told him I'd be back, that he was safe now and we'd come to take him home." She turned and stared back at the darkened room. "They deserved it, Lucas, for what they did to Tyler. For what they did to Cam. For what I know they did to you."

Chris and I stared at her. She'd killed the guards?

"So you came back up to the lounge?" Chris asked. There was no accusation in his voice, no hatred or disgust for what she'd just admitted to doing. "Where did you get the table leg?"

"From me," Ryan said.

Chris and I spun around at the sound of his voice, each of us instinctively moving in front of Carly. "What are you still doing here?" I asked.

"And how much did you hear?" Chris added.

"All the exit doors are locked," Ryan replied. "And I heard everything, but it's not like I didn't already know. I was in there with her." He paused and waved the twins forward. "We all were."

I looked over his shoulder at the twins. Their heads were bowed, their hands fidgeting nervously with the cuffs of their sweatshirts. I silently willed them to look up, to meet my eyes for a fraction of a second, just so I could apologize.

"There were ten of us and five of them, but they had weapons," Ryan continued. "We may have thrown the first punches, but we were smart enough to back off and hide in the corner while everything played out around us.

"Within twenty minutes, the guards had it under control. They were pissed about what we'd done. By the time Carly got here, they were screwing with us, kicking the unconscious and firing their Tasers for no reason. They thought it'd be fun to 'scare some sense into us,' or so they said."

"That's when I hit the guard with the table leg," Carly said. "They didn't hear me come in. It was dark and they were laughing, going on about how they'd done society a favor. Ryan was sitting in the corner, and those two boys over there were hiding behind him. The guards were yanking on Ryan's arms, trying to pull him away from the wall so they could get at the twins."

I turned and looked at the twins. They were shaking, and the entire front of their jeans was soaked with what I presumed was their own piss.

"There was a stun gun sitting on the floor by the door, and I picked it up, not even knowing if it'd work," Carly said, and I remembered the Taser I'd taken off Ms. Tremblay and then lost in the midst of the chaos. "I pulled the trigger, and the guard trying to drag Ryan away fell to the ground and started shaking."

"And that's when *I* hit him with the table leg," Ryan explained.

"And the others?" Chris asked. Ryan had only admitted to killing one guard.

Ryan shrugged, his reply seeming to be an attempt to give us all an alibi rather than answer Chris's question. "It's hard to see in the dark. Who knows how they died or who killed them."

"And what about the guard in the isolation unit?" I asked Carly.

"I wanted to check on Cam, but I knew you wouldn't let

me, would insist we wait for Chris before making our move. So I smashed the lights in the hallway to buy myself some time, confuse you. I didn't mean to kill that guard, just stun him like he did you. But after I did it, he fell down and hit his head."

I turned around and stared at Chris, waiting for him to reveal his role in all this. He just laughed and said, "Don't look at me. My only job was to cut the power permanently, which I did."

I picked up the keys I'd thrown to the ground, turned around, and made my way back to into the lounge, back to the bodies littering the floor.

Ryan and the twins were behind me, whispering questions about what I planned to do and if I would contact the police. I laid my flashlight on the floor by the door, illuminating as much as the room as possible, then motioned for everyone to hand over their lights and any other keys. One by one I put everything back in the guards' utility belts, then motioned for Ryan and the twins to take their boots off and put them back on the guards' feet. As far as I was concerned, none of us had stepped foot in this room.

"No keys, but I found more flashlights," Mrs. Tremblay said as I stepped back into the hall. Her eyes scanned the area in search of the guards and kids I'd told her I was going back for. "Where's everybody else?"

I stood there silently for a second, carefully weighing my words. "There are five dead guards in there. The medic too." I paused and motioned to Ryan and the twins. "The three of us came here looking for keys, and that's where we found these guys. They're the only ones who survived. You can check the lounge yourself if you don't believe me."

"What happened?" Ms. Tremblay asked, looking over my shoulder to see inside the room.

"From the looks of it, the guards panicked and lashed out at anything that moved, including each other." I turned to Ryan, waiting for him to nod in agreement.

"I didn't touch anybody," Ryan said, confirming my lie. "I hid in the corner with these two, hoping someone would eventually come back for us. They didn't touch anybody either."

"It should've been me," Ms. Tremblay said. "It should've been me who made sure you were safe, who got you all out of this room, not Lucas and Chris."

I shrugged. It didn't matter who'd got them out, so long as they were alive.

"I'm sorry about what happened to your brother, Carly," Ms. Tremblay said.

Carly didn't respond, just turned around and walked out of the room after Chris. I knew what she was thinking; my mind was entrenched in the same thought. "Sorry" didn't bring them back. It was only a word, a stupid two-syllable word that held absolutely no power.

THIRTY-EIGHT

Joe was standing by the Bake Shop's outer fence, his hands twisted through the links. The four boys he'd brought with him were fanned out to his left. But not Nick. No, Nick had scaled the fence and was hacking at the razor wire with what looked like a pocketknife.

Joe's eyes skirted over the body slung over my shoulder. I'd gone back for Cam. I'd promised Carly I'd get him out, and after everything that had happened, it seemed like the right thing to do.

Carly was beside me, Chris half holding her up as we shuffled our way to the gate. She'd started crying again the second I'd picked up Cam, the reality of all she'd lost settling in.

"What happened?" Nick dropped to the ground and made his way to the gate too. Struggling under Cam's dead weight, I pressed the keys up against the fence until Nick was able to reach through and snag them. He held them up one by one until Ms. Tremblay nodded, then shoved that key into the lock and pushed the gate wide.

I took one step out into the open and lowered Cam down to the ground by Joe's feet. "I said I'd get him out, and I did."

Joe let out a wail so broken and full of pain that I wondered if his hatred of this facility and everything it stood for ran deeper than I'd originally thought. I should've asked, but to be honest, at that point I really didn't care. I knew he had questions; I could see them brimming in his eyes. I'd explain everything later, when I was hundreds of miles away from this place, away from the memory of Carly's cries and Cam's body hanging there, his lifeless eyes staring up at the ceiling of the place that had ruined us all. But not yet. Adding another layer of agony to an already painful situation would literally kill me.

Joe knelt down beside Cam's body and pressed an ear to his chest, listening for signs of life I knew he'd never find.

"He's gone." I started to sway, mental and physical exhaustion sweeping over me.

"Lucas? You okay?" Nick reached out to steady me.

I shook my head, my legs nearly giving out underneath me. I was so far from okay, it was insane.

"The others—"

"I don't give a shit about the others right now," Nick interrupted. "Tyler was my best friend, and you're his brother. I signed onto this plan for you. Only you. Are *you* okay?"

"No." It was the truth, and it felt amazing to finally admit it. I hadn't been okay since the day I'd found Tyler dead in the backyard, since the day they'd taken him away, and this stupid mission had only made things worse.

"Anne?" Joe stood up and walked toward Ms. Tremblay. "What happened?"

She looked from Joe to me, as if seeking my permission. Or perhaps my forgiveness. I'd give her the words, if that was what she needed, but she'd be an idiot to think it'd help. My forgiveness would never be able to erase her own guilt.

"I'll do anything I can to help you prove that this facility, and all the others, need to be shut down," she said to Joe. "You have my word."

I nodded. But in the end, it was of little consequence to me. I'd pretty much lost everything anyway.

Nick's gaze drifted to the building behind me, and I turned in time to see Ryan emerging from the door. The twins stumbled out behind him, shielding their eyes as they struggled to adjust to the first daylight they'd seen in a while. They were bleeding and bruised, physically holding each other upright.

"Who are they?" Joe asked, reaching for the rifle he'd propped against the fence.

"Kids exactly like me. Exactly like Cam and Tyler. Difference is, they get to go home." I turned my attention to Nick. "I'm ready to go home. We're *all* ready to go home."

EPILOGUE

It never changes. Night after night I relive it all over again. The sounds, the smells, the gut-wrenching panic that eats at my insides until I think I'm going to die. It's easier during the day, when I have school and homework to distract me. But even then, the memory never truly fades; it just tucks itself into the back of my mind, lying in wait until my body gives in and finally falls asleep.

I rub at my eyes and stare down at the blur of words I've scribbled across my paper. It started off as the essay for my college applications, a quick six hundred words on what "sets me apart" from the other applicants. How am I supposed to answer that without scaring the crap out of every admittance counselor?

I slam my laptop closed and sulk out the back door, taking a seat in the exact same lawn chair that Tyler died in. More than once I've found myself here, wondering if there was anything I could've done to save Tyler and struggling to find my own sense of peace. It never comes.

"Hey." The sound of Carly's voice startles me, and I whip my head around, trying for a smile. I know how hard it must be for her most of the time, but day after day she still shows up at my house, asking me how I'm doing in school and talking about her friends. She doesn't ask about Chris or Ryan; it's as if the simple mention of their names will toss her back into the world of darkness she's just recently learned how to escape.

"Bad day?" Carly asks, and I nod. She doesn't need any more explanation than that. She was there; she understands.

"Come here," I say as I hold my arms out wide. She settles into my lap, her tiny hands winding around my neck. This is my favorite time of day, the only time I find peace—Carly in my arms, me knowing that she's safe. That they didn't break her too.

The Bake Shop and the other testing facilities were shut down a month after we got home. Ms. Tremblay kept her promise—she took Joe's information to Washington. To the Government Task Force for Violent Crimes. To the press. She didn't stop until every single one of the facilities was shut down. There is one still physically standing, but its halls are empty; the only people who ever pass through its gates are freelance reporters looking for a story to sell.

And through it all, through the countless interviews she's been forced into and the testimony she's given, Ms. Tremblay has never once sold us out. Never once indicated that Carly, Chris, or I might have had anything to do with the events of that day.

Carly's thumb circles my palm, and I pull her in tighter to my chest. Even if things never go back to how they used to be, even if the memory of that time and all we lost never fades, at least I have her. And right now, she's all I need.

Acknowledgments

This book does not belong solely to Lindsay and I, but rather to the people whose faith in us as authors made it possible. A heartfelt thank you to our agents, Kevan Lyon and Kathleen Rushall, for being our grounding point as we plotted, wrote, and revised this manuscript. To our amazing editor, Brian Farrey-Latz, for seeing the potential in this story concept when it was nothing more than a three-sentence pitch, and Sandy Sullivan, whose keen eye and attention to detail made this book shine. Thanks to our families, whose unwavering support makes all things in our writing world possible. And to our friends and critique partners, Jenni Walsh and Tracey Neithercott, for their long-distance moral support.

© Boule Photography

Trisha Leaver graduated from the University of Vermont with a degree in Social Work. She is a member of SCBWI, the Horror Writers Association, and the Cape Cod Children's Writers. Visit her online at www.trishaleaver.com.

© Alan Klehr

Lindsay Currie graduated from Knox College and is a member of SCBWI, the Horror Writers Association, the YA Scream Queens, and OneFourKidLit, a community of authors with debuts in 2014. Visit her online at www.lindsaycurrie.com.